TRIBES

Part Three of the Convulsive Series

MARCUS MARTIN

ACKNOWLEDGMENTS

With thanks to John Wallis, Alex O'Bryan-Tear, Chris Powell, and Oliver Freeman for your insights and feedback. To Mum, Dad, Charlotte and Tania for your support and love.

Contents

ONE

Freefall

Lucy peered through the night vision goggles and scanned the road. She perceived movement in every shadow, jumped at every waving branch, flinched at the slightest creak. She was exhausted. Freezing. Hungry. Longing for the dawn.

Her disturbed sleep was an uneasy series of nightmarish flashbacks to the hours before; General Whitaker's Jeep tumbling across the tar of Camp Oscar, his broken neck, the swarms of beasts tearing through the convoy. She wondered if they were the only ones to have made it out alive. Major Lopez had vetoed further discussion of the topic as a distraction – as far as he was concerned, their sole aim was to get to DC alive and regroup with whatever remained of the nation's armed forces.

Lucy placed the goggles on her lap and blinked at the darkness. Drifting clouds obscured the moonlight, leaving only scant illumination for the fields and trees. Lucy wished snow could cover the windscreen and simply shut out the world outside. The windows were already covered so it would've completed their camouflage, but Lopez had been adamant: they needed eyes on the road in case another convey passed by on route to the capital. The snow had

1

stopped, anyway, presumably sometime during Jackson's shift, meaning they could stop the intermittent wiper blades and save some precious power. Private Jackson had woken Lucy up thirty minutes ago, plucking Lucy from a guilt-ridden nightmare about her estranged mother, and handing her the goggles all too gladly.

Lucy consulted the dashboard. It was 4:31 AM. Dawn was a long way off. She shivered and rubbed her hands together, blowing onto her numb fingertips. Her breath misted inside the freezing truck. The AC was useless with the engine off, and they had to conserve fuel.

She swiveled in the front passenger seat and looked at the other two. Major Lopez's mouth hung open as he quietly snored. Jackson's lips, by contrast, were pursed, and a frown lingered across her unconscious face.

Lucy's eyes hesitated on the empty driver's seat. She felt a pang of grief. What she'd give to hold her Dan again. To feel his arms around her, his cheek against hers. She played his voice over in her head, imagining him greeting her with the warmth and love they'd shared. Tears filled her eyes. Her hands twitched, remembering the touch of his broken body in the wreckage. It had been so heavy. What were his last words? What would they have been, if she'd been with him at the end? She flinched, swatting her arm, then brushing it furiously as the memory of Dan's disintegration resurfaced like an electric shock. She remembered the flecks of his liquefied flesh spraying her. Lucy broke down, clutching her hair and stifling her sobs in the confines of the static Humvee, trying not to wake the sleeping soldiers.

She grabbed her backpack and pulled out her notepad. Struggling to grip the pen in her frigid fingers, she scrawled by the slender moonlight.

Why me? Why was I the one to live?

She paused and looked at the page. She couldn't see the words, let alone the lines. It didn't matter. All she could see was the train crash.

If I'd been standing anywhere else, I'd be with you now, wherever you are. Maybe oblivion. Anything is better than life without you. I was your Lucy. You were my Dan. And I let you go. I didn't protect you. My soulmate. I failed you.

She thrust the notepad back into her bag and squeezed her eyes shut, stemming the fresh wave of tears. As far as she knew, Dan's father was waiting for them in DC. What could she possibly tell him?

***

BANG.

Lucy awoke with a jolt. Lopez was looming over her, livid.

"Sorry, did I startle you?" he said, aggressively.

"What the fuck?" said Jackson, drowsily, from the back.

Lucy froze. The cold tip of Lopez's pistol was pushing hard up under her chin.

"What's happening?" said Lucy, blinking him into focus. His head was silhouetted in a white glow.

"Ditto that," said Jackson.

"Great question. What *is* happening? We have no idea, because Young here fell asleep on watch," said Lopez, holstering his pistol and taking the driver's seat.

"I'm sorry," said Lucy, sitting up, squinting.

Daylight poured through the windscreen and bounced between the snow-clad windows.

"I don't want to hear 'sorry'. Sorry's too late. Sorry's the sound of us getting killed. Sort your shit out, Young, We're late for DC, and time is critical," said Lopez.

"Lay off, Major, she's just a civvie," said Jackson.

"The hell she is. She's in uniform, she's a soldier now. Time to start acting like one."

"Right, cos that's how it works," said Lucy.

"That's *exactly* how it works. We're at war, Young. In war, civilians die. Soldiers fight. Choose which one you're gonna be, and choose fast, because we don't have room for deadweight. I'm gonna check the house. Jackson, the engine's out. Get it working."

With that Lopez forced the door open, breaking the seal of icy-snow. He climbed out, letting in a blast of frigid air.

"God damned summer Hummers," said Jackson climbing into the driver's seat. She depressed the clutch and toggled the engine switch several times. "Great. Just great. Hope you like pushing, Young," she said. Jackson stuck the gear into second, left the switch on, and hopped out.

Lucy followed her out onto the powdery fresh snow, which formed a panoramic blanket. Daylight bounced between the clouds and the snow. Adjacent to the Humvee was a darkened bungalow. Lopez smashed the glass of the front door and let himself in.

Lucy copied Jackson in kicking snow away from the front of the truck's wheels until they'd created a series of gullies. She followed Jackson to the rear of the vehicle.

4

"Push," grunted Jackson, as the pair leant into the snow-clad vehicle. The Humvee didn't budge.

"Come *on*," groaned Jackson, straining.

Lucy pushed harder still, relying heavily on the traction of her boots. The truck crunched forwards over the powdery snow.

"That's it!" croaked Jackson, wincing with the exertion.

The engine spluttered into life and the truck jolted forwards, now moving under its own power. Jackson tried to chase after it but stopped, bent over, wheezing.

"Get it!" she insisted, motioning Lucy to stop the truck.

Lucy scrambled across the snow, chasing after the trundling vehicle. She hauled herself inside the driver's seat and shoved the gear into neutral. The truck slowed to a halt and Lucy crunched on the handbrake, then revved the gas several times until she was confident the engine wasn't going to falter. She left the engine running and jogged back to Jackson, who was still bent over.

"You OK?" Lucy said, catching up.

"It's nothing," said Jackson, waving her away. "Just low blood sugar and dehydration."

"This oughta help," said Lopez, emerging from the house. He chucked Jackson half a bottle of concentrated orange juice. "Don't drink it all – that's gotta last the three of us," he added.

He had three blankets tucked under his arm, and two large plastic bags – one containing jumbled winter-wear accessories, the other full of empty sports bottles.

"Wrap up," he said, handing Lucy and Jackson a woolly hat each. While the pair rummaged through the bags for scarves and gloves, Lopez popped the Humvee's snow-covered hood and placed three aluminum parcels on top of the engine, before resealing it.

Once wrapped up Lucy copied Jackson, who was filling the sports bottles with snow. They filled the lot while Lopez scraped the Humvee's windows clear. The three of them reconvened inside the truck.

"The road's bearing south-south-east. Ideally, we'll find a freeway which can get us to the nearest city," said Lopez.

"Is that sensible? I thought the convoy was avoiding cities?" said Lucy.

"Look how well that worked out," said Lopez, taking a swig of orange juice and passing it back to Jackson.

"Was that full when you found it?" said Lucy, eyeing up the juice.

"You saying I took more than my share?" said Lopez.

"It's just a question," said Lucy, receiving the carton from Jackson.

"How about next time you go find provisions, then *you* can answer that question yourself," retorted Lopez.

"I'mma use the bathroom before we move out," said Jackson.

"Me too," said Lucy, wiping her mouth on her sleeve.

She followed Jackson to the abandoned house, leaving Lopez to further consult the compass.

The house was modest inside. Lucy explored, tentatively, while waiting for Jackson to finish. The décor was several decades out of date. A bed with a black duvet but no sheet on the mattress. Posters of classic rock bands on the walls. In the lounge there was a faded linen sofa and a hamburger phone. Dark patches stained the sofa, and clothes lay strewn across the cushions.

"All yours," said Jackson, leaving the bathroom.

Lucy entered, holding her breath. The room didn't smell, but the toilet seat was warm. Steam rose from Jackson's urine, which was seeping into the toilet's frozen water.

Lucy defecated then instinctively went to flush. No water was released, but the handle felt warm. Lucy prized off the plastic cistern lid and peered inside, immediately feeling the warmer air rise up to greet her. Growing out of the water pipe and stretching onto the cistern walls were short, fine blades of bleached grass, tightly packed together. They looked damp. Lucy peered closer. It grew as far down the pipe as she could see. A rattling sound pricked her ears. There was a distinct rhythm to it, like something scuttling. There was a loud clang and the cistern shook. The scuttling got louder, and faster. A second clang. Lucy shoved the lid over the cistern and ran back to the truck.

"Drive!" she insisted.

Lopez released the handbrake and hit the gas, propelling them forwards.

"What's going on?" said Jackson, following Lucy's gaze to the rear of the truck.

"There's something in there," said Lucy.

"A beast?" said Jackson, grabbing her rifle.

"Something else," said Lucy.

"What?"

"I didn't wait to find out," said Lucy, as the house shrank behind them.

"You see that?" said Jackson, squinting down the sight of her barrel.

Snow sprayed up from the front of the house as something dark scuttled down the path onto the road. Lucy fumbled for the binoculars as the creature darted across their tracks and burrowed into the neighboring virgin snow. The snow spraying ceased, but cracks and ridges would appear in the snow as the creature scoured the house's surroundings, moving sideways across the road in a narrow zig zag. Jackson slumped back into her seat. She looked pale. Lucy continued staring until the creature's tracks were out of sight.

***

They'd been driving for almost an hour when Lucy broke the silence. There'd been no further sign of the scuttling creature, but a car had caught her eye.

"Pull over," she urged, as they passed the stationary vehicle.

"If we stop to check out abandoned vehicles we'll never make it to DC," replied Lopez.

"There's a gun in there," she insisted.

"What?" said Lopez.

"The driver shot themselves," said Lucy, eyeing up the car's blood-splattered windows.

"How'd you know it wasn't a beast?" said Jackson.

"Because none of the windows are smashed. Now pull over," said Lucy.

Lopez backed up until they reached the abandoned car. Lucy and Jackson climbed out. There were no tire marks in the vehicle's wake. Snow covered the bottom half of the windows, while the frosted top half was stained with brown blotches. Lucy prized the cold handle open, revealing the frost-bitten corpse of the driver inside. Dried flecks of brain and bone had frozen to the roof, where the bullet had left the man's skull. A small pile of snow sat on the man's shoulders and hair, beneath the hole in the roof. The man's pale skin had turned dark blue, and was chapped. His eyelids were closed, and his mouth hung open where he'd inserted the gun. He must've been around forty.

Lucy prized the gun from the man's rigid, mottled hand. The frozen body could have been anything from a week to a couple of months old. She checked the glove compartment and pocketed the bullets, tissues, and mints therein. Jackson's sweep of the other seats found nothing useful, so the pair checked out the trunk.

There was a car manual, a spare tire, bag of fertilizer, and a shovel. Jackson grabbed the shovel and Myles's head split open with a crack. He fell to the ground and Dan smashed down on his head again, and again, hammering the flat blade into her boss's skull until the man's head was but a bloodied pulp. The road was smeared in blood and brain tissue, soon to be baked by the Californian sun. Myles's knife lay discarded by his body. They had to get rid of the evidence before anyone saw, but Dan was going into shock. She shook him. "Look at me. *Look at me!* You're OK! Take his legs," she said, sliding her hands under Myles's arms. She could feel the warmth of his body through her rubber gloves. They had to get him in the compressor before anyone saw.

The trunk slammed shut.

"Young? You OK?" said Jackson, eyeing her warily.

Lucy realized she'd recoiled several paces from the car.

"You went weird," said Jackson, her eyebrow cocked.

"I'm fine, let's get back to the truck," croaked Lucy.

"Look on the upside, he died doing what he loved," said Jackson, gesturing to the driver with a bitter laugh.

Lucy's mouth was dry. The traumatized look on Dan's face lingered on her mind. She climbed back into the Humvee, dully registering the warmth inside. A strong and welcome scent greeted her – one that she hadn't smelled in months.

"Breakfast is served, people," said Lopez.

He handed her and Jackson a foil package each – they were piping hot. Jackson unwrapped hers eagerly and let out a gasp of delight. Lucy copied, her hunger bringing her brain back into the present. Nestled in the folds of creased metal were steaming flakes of tuna.

"How did you-?" said Lucy, tearing off a glove and grabbing the hot fish with her fingers, shoveling it into her mouth and venting the steam with each ravenous chew.

"Don't tell me this is your first carbeque?" said Lopez, setting the Humvee in motion.

Jackson beckoned Lucy for the juice.

"Finally!" cheered Lopez, pointing to a road sign up ahead. "Welcome to Route 56, folks. Let's hope it's our lucky number."

Once Jackson had finished eating she took over driving from Lopez, who tucked into his own foil package. A plume of smoke caught Lucy's eye. It was rising from the chimney of one of the isolated roadside homes.

"Should we stop?" she said.

No-one replied, and Jackson drove by. More empty homes dotted the road, but within a few miles there was another plume of smoke.

As the houses became more regular, a second sign greeted them. *Welcome to Madison.*

The number of active chimneys was increasing too. Lucy counted a few each minute they drove, but they only made up a tiny fraction of the otherwise deserted homes they were passing.

"Look!" said Lucy, pointing ahead.

A man in his fifties was leaving his driveway. He was on foot, pushing a supermarket cart onto the snowy sidewalk. The cart's wheels had been adapted with spikes that gripped the powdery terrain. Inside it were some tinned goods. The man looked up, hearing the truck. He released the cart and waved, furiously, becoming increasingly animated the closer they got.

"We should stop, right?" said Lucy.

"And say what?" shrugged Jackson, driving past the man.

The stranger jumped up and down in a desperate bid to flag them down. Lucy watched as he tried to run after them but his pace in the snow was pitiful. He gave up quickly and stared, with drooped shoulders, as they left.

"Jackson's right. We've got no business with these people. There'll be more like him. No point stopping for one, if you can't stop for them all," said Lopez.

Lucy took in the town. Heads were appearing in the windows of chimney-using homes, drawn by the rumbling engine. A few people dashed out onto their drives, trying to catch the visitors.

The homes gave way to retail units and factories as the center became more urbanized. "Bingo," said Lopez, spotting a mall up ahead. Jackson pulled into the parking lot. The superstore's front windows were smashed, and several inches of snow lay inside.

"We get in, we get out. Be quick - people know we're here. Find what food and drink you can, and meet me back here in no more than five minutes," said Lopez.

"Where are you going?" asked Lucy, as they clambered out.

"Bathroom," said Lopez, stepping over the shards of glass and making a beeline towards the men's room.

"You wanna push or grab?" said Jackson, swinging an empty cart around.

"Not sure there's much to grab, but I'll try," said Lucy, eyeing up the shelves. The store was around forty percent full. Lightbulbs, greeting cards, DVDs, air fresheners were all in abundance, but the food shelves were barren.

"There's gotta be something," said Jackson, as they hurried down the aisles, doing lengths of the store until they reached the far end. The yield was depressing. Cooking oil, tea bags, cat food, and several bottles of ketchup. They reached the edge of the checkout area. Lucy glanced at the registers and wondered if they had any cash left in them, or if some couple had robbed the place, back when money was useful.

"We should check out back," said Lucy, looking for a staff door.

Jackson followed with the cart. Skylights illuminated the warehouse, in spite of the layer of snow. The place was a mess. Torn cardboard littered the floor, where discarded boxes spewed their contents. Rolls of toilet paper, freezer bags, and clothes, covered the concrete.

"You see that?" said Jackson, pointing to the skylight overhead.

Lucy looked up, squinting. Encircling the frame was dark purple algae, which grew outwards from the light in a radial fashion as it colonized the surrounding ceiling.

Three sharp whistle blasts interrupted her speculation.

"Crap," said Jackson, swinging her rifle off her shoulder. "On me!"

Lucy rushed after Jackson, back through the store, trying to keep pace with the cart. The whistle blasts repeated. They were coming from the parking lot, where a crowd had surrounded the Humvee. The people were wrapped in thick layers of clothes. Many wore skis and held ski poles – some of the kits were real, others notably home-made. Three people were wearing full ice-hockey uniforms, with hockey sticks slung over their shoulders. The range in height and breadth suggested the crowd spanned ages and sexes.

"I make eleven. Follow my lead," said Jackson, as they crossed into the lot.

Lopez's voice carried as they approached. His tone was strained.

"We *can't* take you. No, I don't have any more information. I've told you already, there's a mustering operation at DC. We will come back for you. The army will come back for you. I don't know when. My guess is spring."

"Make way!" Jackson called, interrupting Lopez's efforts. She grabbed the front of Lucy's cart and sprinted towards the truck, dragging Lucy with it. The people nearest them moved out of the way just in time as Jackson skidded into the side of the Hummer.

"Young, cover me," Jackson ordered, as she pulled the door open and began throwing the supplies into the truck.

Lucy turned to face the crowd.

"Please, help us," said an older woman, squeezing Lucy's arms desperately.

"Take us with you," said one of the hockey players, edging closer, his young eyes wide with hope behind the mesh of his helmet.

"Shit," said Jackson, abandoning the truck and pushing her way through the crowd to the far side. A child had opened the door opposite and was stealing the cans Jackson had loaded. Jackson chased after the child, who doubled back and retreated towards their parent.

A rattling drew Lucy's head back to the front. People were rifling through the cart and stealing the remaining items. Lucy tried to shove their hands away but in doing so relinquished her grip on the cart. The group wrenched the cart away and surrounded Lucy.

"Back up!" she cried, trying to imitate Lopez's authority as half a dozen hands patted her uniform down, groping for pockets. "Hey!" she cried, trying to fend them off. The old woman had opened Lucy's breast pocket and was pulling out the tissues and mints. The young hockey players was raiding another pocket, pulling out wound dressings. Another hand found her compass. "Get off!" Lucy cried, but the more she tried to bat away the clawing hands, the more frenzied they became.

"Young, close the door!" called Lopez.

Lucy realized she'd left the loading door unguarded. A second child had pulled it open and was reaching inside. As Lucy grabbed

14

the child's shoulder, a strong adult hand wrapped itself around her own wrist, pulling her back. More hands scratched at her pockets. They were becoming rougher; shoving her as they searched.

"Jackson!" cried Lopez, his tone urgent.

A stranger had climbed into the driver's seat of the Humvee, and was looking for the ignition key.

"Jackson, now!" Lopez screamed.

Jackson darted to the truck and grabbed the man, hurling him out of the truck and throwing him backwards onto the ground.

"Bastard!" cried a woman from the front, punching Lopez hard in the face.

Lopez chopped her in the larynx, sending the woman staggering back, spluttering. He pulled out his handgun and fired a shot into the air. The crowd flinched, ducking down on mass and scattering backwards.

"Back up, *now!*" cried Lopez, aiming at the hockey player nearest him, who was reaching for her stick.

The engine sprung into life. Jackson was in the driving seat. "Young, get in!" cried Lopez, rotating his aim across the crowd as individuals edged closer in alternation.

Lucy scrambled into the back of the car and slammed the door. Lopez leapt into the front. The crowd rushed towards the Humvee and thumped the sides, slamming it with their gloves, beating it with ski poles, creating the effect of a hailstorm striking the truck. Lucy's door clicked open. She grabbed the handle and pulled back as hard as she could, but the outsider was stronger. With a roar of the engine the Humvee lurched forwards, throwing Lucy's assailant off-balance, and slamming the door shut. Jackson pulled out of the parking lot at speed, skidding around the snow-covered corner onto the main boulevard.

Lucy looked back. The women who had punched Lopez was on her knees tending to a motionless man on his back – the man Jackson had thrown to the ground. A pool of blood seeped from his head, turning the surrounding white ice to crimson. Two members of the crowd pulled the shopping cart level with the man and bent down to lift him.

More skiers were arriving at the mall, following the Humvee's original tracks in the snow. From the opposite side of the boulevard, a woman was hurrying across the snow towards them, wobbling in her snowshoes. One by one the strangers gave up and watched despondently as the Humvee escaped them all.

Lucy's heart continued to pound as they crossed a river bridge and left the town behind.

"What the *hell* was that, Young?" cried Lopez. "That's your idea of covering a door? My *god!*"

Lucy's blood boiled.

"How about you go fuck yourself, Major," she said, balling her fist.

"What did you just say*?*" said Lopez.

"I have zero training. You guys conscripted me barely three days ago, after I was nearly raped and killed by some *psychopaths*. Then you load me into a truck and drive into a massacre at Camp Oscar. And now the fact that you couldn't handle a bunch of civilians is apparently *my* fault? Go to hell."

"Oh, I get it. Because you've had a rough time, it's on everyone else to look after you, is that it? I got news for you, that's not how conflict situations work."

"Don't patronize me," snapped Lucy.

"Then pull your god damned weight. I don't mean with more bullshit experiments that get good people killed, I mean get your head in the game like a real soldier."

"Like you?"

"That's it. You're officially demoted, gimme me that slider right now," said Lopez, pointing at her captain's insignis.

"With *pleasure*," laughed Lucy, tearing the slider off and tossing it at Lopez.

"You wanna go it alone, Young? Be my guest. Otherwise, you will shut the hell up, and you will learn discipline, fast, before you get the rest of us killed."

"Please, Major, teach me everything you know. It was clearly of such *value* to the hundreds of people who died last night."

"This is unacceptable. Jackson, pull over. I want Young out of this vehicle now."

Jackson continued driving.

"Jackson?"

"She's the reason both of us are alive, Major," said Jackson, keeping her eyes fixed on the road.

"I'm giving you an order, Jackson," said Lopez, fuming.

Jackson said nothing.

"I see how it is," said Lopez, his eyes bulging.

"I'm on your side, Major. But I'm on hers too. We're a unit. You taught me that," said Jackson.

Lopez said nothing, and a silence fell over the car. Lucy hugged her sides and stared out of the window as the road shadowed the meandering route of the river. Her daily water-gathering routine seemed a long time ago. Jackson kept their speed moderate, conserving fuel and keeping control on the snow-covered roads.

Lucy's torso was bruised from the rough pickpocketing crowd. Her mind flashed back to the mob in San Francisco. To the people chasing the train as it pulled out of the station. Arms extended. Running. Reaching. Falling. Gone.

***

"Gas," said Jackson, some time later.

They'd picked up a deserted highway headed for Cincinnati, but fuel was running low.

"Halle-freakin-lujah," said Lopez.

"We'll see," said Jackson, turning off the freeway and down the icy slip road.

Traffic signals hung above the deserted intersection, covered in an inch of snow. Icicles grew from the lights like a beard, dripping in the morning sun. Jackson followed the sign to the station and whistled, impressed.

"Love what they've done with the place," she chimed.

The station was a charred shell. Scorch marks stretched to every inch of the tattered structure. Along the ground, fallen roof panels poked through the snow, in between burned out cars which had lost their windows. The pumps had been obliterated in the explosion, along with much of the adjacent store. In front of the wreckage, facing the road, was a large hand-painted sign that simply read: *GAS*, with an arrow pointing the other way.

Jackson hooked a U-turn and they retraced their route. At the intersection they crossed under the freeway, towards the other services. The second gas station was intact, and had a single car on the forecourt: a small Chevy hatchback. Three men climbed out, wrapped in thick layers of clothes. The foremost man signaled Jackson to stop. His navy tracksuit looked stuffed and misshapen, like he was wearing multiple layers. He wore a black scarf and red fleece hat, which contrasted against his pale cheeks. The second man wore a deerstalker hat and brown duffle coat with an upturned collar. The coat covered his ear lobes down to his shins, where his hiking boots took over. The third man, by contrast, was clad in designer skiwear. He sported a coordinated ensemble of snow boots, charcoal-grey ski pants, and a two-tone grey-black jacket, with the hood pulled up. Jackson, Lopez, and Lucy climbed out in their matching fatigues and met the men on the forecourt.

"You guys selling this stuff?" said Jackson.

"Nah, we here for the ambience," said the man in the red hat. The other two men guffawed at this.

"How much?" said Jackson, without smiling.

"What you got?" replied the duffle coat guy.

"We're with the US Army," said Lopez, straightening up his uniform.

"Technically, we with the US Probation Service, so let's call it even," said the man in the red hat.

"He means like we was their number one customers, you know what I'm saying?" laughed the man in skiwear.

"They got it, Alfonse. You over-explained it again," sighed Red Hat.

"We're freezing our asses off here and we need to get to DC. You gonna give us fuel or what?" snapped Jackson.

"Alfonse, remember that sign you put up out front – what does it say?" said Duffle Coat.

"It says 'gas'," said Alfonse.

"Huh. So I'm wondering why these clowns think we some kinda charity," said Duffle Coat.

"You're telling me you won't even support your own army in a crisis?" said Lopez.

"That would be a yes," said Red Hat.

"So patriotism is truly dead," said Lopez, despondently.

"Naw, it's still alive, man. It's everyone else that croaked," chuckled Alfonse.

"Screw these guys. There'll be other gas stations," said Jackson.

"You sure about that, baby?" said Duffle Coat.

"Who you callin' 'baby'?" said Jackson.

"You," said Duffle Coat.

"You didn't call him 'baby'," said Jackson, gesturing to Lopez.

"Nah, I call him 'cupcake'," said Duffle Coat.

Alfonse and Red Hat howled with laughter.

Lucy pulled out a handgun.

"Woah, cool it!" cried the tallest man, as all three men drew their weapons, prompting Lopez and Jackson to do the same. All laughter was gone, and eyes were on Lucy's gun. It was the one she'd scavenged from the abandoned car.

"Young, what the hell are you doing?" fumed Lopez.

"This gun's in good condition. We'll give you it if you fill our tank," said Lucy, ignoring Lopez and focusing on the men.

20

Red Hat took the pistol and inspected it.

"This buys you ten gallons," he declared.

Lucy reached into her vest pocket a retrieved a handful of bullets.

"Alright. Twenty gallons," Red Hat conceded.

"Not enough. We need more – we're in a Hummer for Christ's sake," said Jackson.

Lucy reached into the car and pulled out three bottles of ketchup.

"You kidding me?" said Red Hat, scowling.

"There's five hundred calories in each bottle. Right now I'm guessing that's about a day's worth of calories for each of you, and I don't see many other folk lining up to give you food," said Lucy.

"You got any mayo? I don't like ketchup," said Alfonse.

Duffle Coat elbowed him.

"Yo, sidebar," said Red Hat, stepping to one side to consult with Alfonse and Duffle Coat.

Lopez grabbed Lucy by the arm, firmly, and turned his back on the group.

"You wanna give us some warning next time, before you pull a gun on total strangers?" he hissed.

"You said you wanna get to DC. I'm getting us to DC," said Lucy, shaking him off.

"You had *no* idea how they were gonna react. That move could've got us killed," said Lopez.

"How history would've missed us," said Lucy, staring him the eye.

Lopez glared at her.

"We good here?" said Jackson, leaning in to their confrontation.

"Yeah, we're the dream," said Lopez, walking away.

Jackson waited until he was a few paces away, then leaned in to Lucy.

"I get it, you're going through some stuff. Been there. But the Major's right. Don't be a loose cannon," said Jackson. She gave Lucy two pats on the back then followed after the Major, who was doing a lap of the Hummer.

Lucy's fists clenched. She felt herself quiver with rage. Some 'stuff'? These people had *no idea* what she'd been through. They hadn't survived alone, for months, carving out a brutal existence amidst the clutches of winter. They hadn't lost their loved ones the way she had. Yet here they were, controlling her, telling her how to survive, how to negotiate, how to *grieve*.

"Yo, we got a question about the ketchup," said Duffle Coat, invading Lucy's private rage.

"Take the damned bottles, coat man. Whatever your question is, my answer is: Take. The. Bottles," said Lucy.

"Or we'll use your twenty gallons to drive to another gas station and trade it with them," added Jackson.

"A'ight, Bottles will get you five more gallons," said Red hat.

"I reckon I could eat one of you with enough ketchup," said Alfonse, nudging Duffle Coat.

"Man, you'd be too busy choking on your own bullshit to swallow either of us," Duffle Coat replied.

"Yo, we good. Serve 'em up," ordered Red Hat.

Alfonse and Duffle Coat crouched down and pushed against the hood of their car until the vehicle rolled back several yards, revealing a fuel hatch in the ground. They retrieved some equipment from the car, then set about work.

"You guys run a gas station but you wheel your own car?" said Jackson.

"Waste not, want not," said Red Hat.

"You've got no idea how much fuel's left in there, have you?" said Lucy.

Red Hat scoffed.

Alfonse levered the hatch open, and Duffle Coat knelt down beside it. He pulled a buff over his mouth and nose, then lowered a bailer bucket inside. The hatch was narrow – only a few coffee cups wide. Duffle Coat continued lowering the bailer bucket, releasing the coiled cable from around his shoulder inch by inch over the course of a minute.

"How deep does that thing go?" said Lopez, re-joining the group.

"'Bout thirty feet," said Red Hat.

"How many gallons is your bucket?" said Jackson.

"Five or so."

"Jesus, we're gonna be here all day," Jackson protested.

"Fine by me," said Red Hat. "I ain't go nowhere to be. How about you, Earl, you got somewhere to be?"

"Nah. I had a date but she cancelled cos of the world ending five months ago," said Duffle Coat.

"Quit yankin' us around and hurry it up," said Lopez, impatiently.

"Slow's the only way, boss. Otherwise you excite the fumes. Then boom," said Duffle Coat.

"Why haven't you mechanized this? You could easily rig up a portable generator to power the pumps?" said Jackson.

"You remember the other gas station? The last gang tried just that. That was a bad day for those boys. Great day for us, though. Business really picked up after they exploded themselves," said Red Hat.

"You're telling me *you* guys are the smart ones? That's depressing," said Jackson.

Duffle Coat finished reeling up the first bucket-full. Alfonse placed a jerry can with a cut-off-top beneath it. Duffle Coat decanted the fuel, and Alfonse ported it over to the Humvee, where he tipped it into the tank.

The process was repeated five more times, during which Lucy resorted to doing star jumps to keep warm. Eventually, the order was complete, and Lucy handed the gang their payment.

"Pleasure doing business with you," said Red Hat, loading the bullets into the handgun.

"See you round," said Lucy.

"Word of advice. Don't go into the city. All kinds of crap going on in there. Just go around – use the beltway," Red Hat added, pointing to the intersection from which they'd come.

"Can you be more specific?" said Lucy.

"Yeah. Ask me how many cousins I got left in Cincinnati," he said.

"How many?" asked Lucy.

"One," said Red Hat.

"OK…" said Lucy.

"It used to be two. Ah, I should have said that bit first," mused Red Hat.

"I used to have, like, fifteen, but they all died in the virus thing," said Alfonse.

"'*Like*' fifteen?" said Duffle Coat.

"It's a lot of cousins to keep track of," shrugged Alfonse.

"We've wasted enough time here already, let's go," said Lopez.

Lucy opened the driver's door and climbed into the Humvee.

"I think Jackson should drive," said Lopez, holding the door ajar.

Lucy wrenched it from his grip and slammed the door shut. She fastened her seatbelt and flicked the engine on. Lopez climbed into the passenger seat beside her, glaring at her. Jackson buckled up in the back.

"Recommend us to your friends!" called Red Hat, as Lucy pulled away.

The gas station and the three probationers disappeared from view. The Humvee approached the intersection.

"What's that?" said Jackson, pointing out of the side window.

A man was running towards them from several hundred yards away. He was waving his arms desperately, slipping and stumbling as he scrambled across the snow. Behind him was an abandoned car. The swerving tire tracks looked fresh, and the driver's door was open.

"Creature sighted, hook a right!" said Lopez, binoculars raised, pointing beyond the man.

"You mean leave him?" said Lucy.

"We can't risk losing another engagement. And even if we *did* help, we don't even have enough food as it is," snapped Lopez.

"No way. I listened to you in Madison and you were wrong," said Lucy.

"Creature's closing, Young get us out of here!" barked Lopez.

"We're the US Army, and that's a US citizen," said Lucy, spinning the Humvee around to face the desperate man and hit the gas. The Humvee jostled as it picked up speed.

"Listen to me, Young, we just lost a whole company to these creatures, we need to get to DC alive so we can fight back *in numbers*. If we engage in knee-jerk, emotional fights we won't make it, we have to be disciplined," implored Lopez, shouting over the engine.

Lucy tightened her grip on the wheel and accelerated towards the stumbling man.

"Young, abort!" cried Lopez.

The running man tripped once again. The beast was closing in. The man rolled onto his side, cradling one hand, and scrambled backwards.

"Cover us!" cried Lucy.

She hit the brakes and skidded around, putting the Humvee side-on between the man and the charging creature. Lopez and Jackson flung open their doors and fired on the beast.

Lucy banged on the window and screamed at the man to get in but he scrambled further backwards, his face awash with panic. She threw open the driver's door and leapt out. She ran across the snow, grabbed the man by the shoulders, and hauled him to his feet. Still gripping his coat, she rushed the man towards the vehicle.

"Look out!" cried the man, pointing to the side.

Lucy spun around. A creature had flanked them. It was closing in on the pair of them. She shoved the stranger towards the Humvee and turned to the advancing beast. Setting her feet wide apart, Lucy dug her boots into the snow, blocking the creature's path to the fleeing man. She fumbled for her gun but she couldn't release the holster. The creature was just yards away, bearing down upon her with each great bound.

Lucy looked up and stared at the beast as it prepared for its final leap. The world suddenly slowed and an immense sense of calm washed over her. She stopped reaching for the pistol. Everything suddenly made sense. Lopez and Jackson's gunshots faded to a distant crackle. She noticed the utter tranquility of the snow-dusted city. The mountain-crisp air. The beauty of the creature's lean, muscular design. The richness of its thick, polar fur. The precision of its gait as it bounded towards her. She closed her eyes and pictured Dan's face.

Snow sprayed across her cheek. The creature skidded to a halt just feet from her. Retching and sniffing punctuated its snarls. Lucy opened her eyes. The creature's teeth were bared. It pawed the ground frenetically. Its tail was raised like a periscope and darted around as the embedded black eyeball searched for a way past.

Six rounds tore into the creature, sending it collapsing into a heap with a single whimper.

"Young, get in the fucking truck!" screamed Jackson, her rifle trained on the dead beast.

Lucy came out of her stupor and she regarded the dying creature afresh, suddenly cognizant of the teeth and claws amidst its crumpled mass. A shiver rippled across each of her vertebrae. A long, protracted howl emanated from an alley and echoed around the street. Lucy turned to the vehicle and her heart skipped a beat. A series of crimson dots stained the ice beneath, marking the stranger's path to the Humvee.

A second howl answered the first.

Lucy leapt into the driver's seat and hit the gas.

"Jackson, I think he's bleeding!" she cried, as they sped towards the freeway.

"Holy shit," cried Jackson, seeing the blood drips before the stranger.

"You gotta make it stop," called Lucy.

"More are following us!" called Lopez, as he continued firing pistol shots from the window.

Jackson tore a strip of fabric from one of the scarves and stuffed it into the man's palm.

"Squeeze," she instructed.

"There's paste in my backpack, get it on quickly," called Lucy, swerving around an abandoned car in the middle of the lane.

Jackson dabbed the man's blood away and slathered paste over his cut. She wound the bandaged tight, making him yelp.

"Lose the rags!" called Lucy.

Jackson finished mopping the blood drops from the floor and threw the bloodied scarf from the window.

"Jackson, I could use some help!" called Lopez.

She joined him at the window and fired upon the pack in bursts. But the creatures weaved and crossed paths as they ran, leaping erratically to dodge the shots.

"They're flanking us," cried Lopez.

In a burst of speed, the pack pulled level with the speeding truck, all grouping on one side. The pack leader took several more great strides and began to overtake the Humvee.

"It's a trap, hold on," cried Lucy. She gripped the steering wheel and turned into the leader's path, forcing the creature to skid out of the way.

The truck ricocheted off one of the smaller beasts, jolting as the creature went under the wheels. The rest of the pack fell back, but continued the pursuit. Jackson and Lopez covered alternate windows, felling two beasts, and forcing the pack into a streamlined charge directly behind the truck.

"Major, grenade!" called Jackson.

Lopez tore the pin from his final grenade and held it out of the window, close to the body of the truck. He released the trigger, then dropped it into the snow. A second later, the detonation engulfed half of the pack in a fireball.

The flash drew Lucy's eye to right-hand mirror, where limbless beasts writhed in agony, their fur ablaze.

"Four left," cried Jackson, covering the opposite side.

Lucy sped down the freeway. As the buildings waned, giving way to fields, Jackson ceased firing.

"They're stopping!" she cried.

Lucy watched in the mirror. The beasts had come to a halt. Lucy stared at the four creatures. They stood in a line and stared at the Humvee, as it rushed away from the city.

***

Lucy checked the rear-view mirror. Jackson was slumped in the back of the Humvee. She looked grey, and was sweating.

"Jackson?" repeated Lucy, louder.

"Huh?" said Jackson, waking with a start.

"Are you OK?"

"I'm fine. I just need to rest a bit," she replied.

"You've been out for two hours," said Lopez.

"She doesn't look fine," said the stranger.

His head was shaven at the sides, and backcombed on top, where a slick of thick grey-black hair swept over his scalp. He had a single stud earring, and crease lines across his forehead. His stubble was patchy – it left his cheeks bare, and his fledgling moustache was isolated from the hairs on his chin. He winter jacket had fake fur lining and smelled of cigarettes. Lucy guessed he was around forty.

Since escaping Cincinnati she and Lopez had established few details about their new ward. Lopez, openly resentful of the man, had declined to ask questions, and Lucy had similarly lost her desire to engage. All they knew was that he was Canadian, and he owed them his life.

"To be candid, she looks like hell," the stranger added, still frowning at Jackson.

"New guy, shut up. No-one's asking you," said Lopez, briefly breaking his vow of silence.

"My name's Maurice," said the Canadian.

Lopez ignored him and passed back a candy bar to Jackson, which they'd scavenged from a diner while she was sleeping. "Hey, soldier, you gotta keep eating," he insisted, but she'd drifted off again.

"New guy, unwrap this and hold it to her lips," ordered Lopez.

"My name's—" began the Canadian.

"Your name is whatever the hell I say it is. Understood? You're in my company now, which means my rules."

Lucy snorted.

"Trouble in paradise?" said the Canadian.

"Shut your mouth and feed Jackson," ordered Lopez.

The Canadian obliged.

"Don't mind the Major, he gets cranky when people remind him the army's not real anymore," said Lucy.

"She speaks! How about that," said Lopez.

"That's rich from the guy who stonewalled me for two hours. Such professional behavior from the 'Major'," said Lucy.

"You're still alive, Young. Consider that proof of my professionalism. Now how about you explain yourself," said Lopez.

"Nothing to explain," said Lucy.

"Bullshit," said Lopez.

"We got attacked. We escaped. That's about it," said Lucy.

"How about we start with the bit where you disobeyed a direct order and drove us *into* danger," said Lopez.

"You were going to let Maurice die," said Lucy.

"Good to know," said the Canadian.

"That was *my* call to make. When one person can't be trusted to follow orders in a crisis, the whole group is in jeopardy," said Lopez, seething.

"Got it," said Lucy.

"That right there – that's what I'm talking about. A complete disregard for the survival of anyone in this vehicle. That's it, isn't it? You've given up."

"If I've given up I wouldn't still be alive," said Lucy.

"You're alive because of Jackson. You froze back in the city – up against that beast. I saw it. One minute you were rescuing the Canadian, and the next minute you're standing out in the open, palms stretched out, waiting to be killed," said Lopez.

"I was reaching for my gun," said Lucy.

"Bullshit. You lost your nerve like a damned rookie," fumed Lopez.

"It must be hard for you, having to work with amateurs," said Lucy, blithely.

"Frankly, Young, it is. So don't be a liability. You wanna make it through this, keep your shit together," said Lopez.

"Thanks, I wish I'd thought of that. It just hadn't occurred to me to try," said Lucy.

She brought the Humvee to an abrupt stop.

"That could be a problem," said Lopez, peering through the windscreen.

The road ahead forked into two distinct, parallel bridges – one for each direction of traffic. The eastward section had entirely collapsed, so Lucy pulled them around to the westbound lane.

The remaining bridge was riddled with vast holes and cracks in the tar, each at least a meter across.

"We'd better check this out on foot," said Lopez.

"We? So now you *do* want the rookie's help?" said Lucy.

"All I've ever asked for is your help, Young, but somehow all I've gotten back so far is a lot of wildcard bullshit. Consider this your second chance," said Lopez, climbing out.

Lucy hesitated for a moment and looked at the Major, who was pulling his collar closer around his neck as the cold breeze bit. For so long, she'd been answerable only to herself. This would take some adjusting to. His complaint wasn't entirely baseless, she conceded, but that didn't save him from being a rank-loving asshole.

Lucy exited the truck. Cautiously, the pair approached the bridge. Holes of different sizes revealed the rushing river several meters below. Some holes were circular, others were more like streaks and teardrops in shape.

"No way is that gonna hold a Hummer. We need to find another way round," said Lucy.

"Agreed. Let's double back to the freeway interchange – what was it, couple of miles?" said Lopez.

A familiar, blood-curdling screech rang through the winter air. Lucy's heart froze. Her eyes fell upon the long road from which they'd come. A colossus staggered out from the adjoining field onto the freeway.

"What the hell is that!" yelled the Canadian, as Lucy and Lopez scrambled back into the Humvee.

"Sshh!" insisted Lucy.

"What's going on?" said Jackson, drowsily.

Lopez grabbed his binoculars.

"Has it seen us?" Lucy whispered.

The creature stumbled onto the road a few hundred meters from their position. Its arms were flailing wildly.

"You tell me," said Lopez, thrusting them into Lucy's hands.

She looked intently. The creature was breath-taking. Its great body was covered in white and grey scales, but flashes of color were bursting across its coral-like wings. Its scorpionesque tail twitched, its usual range of motion constricted. The tip was withered, producing sporadic jets of acid which burned through the snow and into the tar beneath. The creature's upper arms were reaching above its head, swatting. The behemoth's bulbous eyes were gone, leaving two, dark sockets carved into its face. The titan flailed around, swiping at the birds which dodged with ease. They took turns to dive bomb the behemoth. Each attack prompted a flash of color across its skin, further breaking its camouflage.

"The birds - they've blinded it," gasped Lucy.

The creature lurched forwards and broke into a run. Its lower fist smashed through a row of fence posts as it lashed out in pain. The flock of pursuing birds was growing in number – they were easily visible without the binoculars.

"It's coming this way!" cried the Canadian.

"Everybody out – to the bridge, now!" ordered Lopez.

Lucy grabbed her backpack and leapt out. Jackson followed but fell straight to her knees. Lucy threw Jackson's arm over her shoulder and heaved the woman to her feet. The pair staggered towards the bridge.

"Hurry!" called Lopez, as the ground reverberated with the titan's approaching bounds.

Maurice was already half-way across, darting between the holes and cracks.

A splash of acid landed on the Humvee, melting through the trunk. More drops began to fall across the road, burning through the tar, which fizzed and smoldered as it disintegrated.

Lopez led the way, beckoning Lucy and Jackson to follow. Lucy hurried Jackson to the lip of the bridge, and took her to the side, where she guided Jackson's hand onto the railing. Jackson staggered forwards, leaning heavily into the mesh. The flecks of acid were getting nearer – reaching beyond the road and onto the bridge where they began to burn new holes and enlarge others.

Jackson halted abruptly. The mesh barrier was gone, and the floor with it.

"You've gotta jump," said Lopez.

"I can't make that," said Jackson.

"You have to!" cried Lucy. She grabbed Jackson's uniform, creating two tight bunches above her waist and shoulders, and rocked Jackson in preparation. "Push off on three," Lucy reiterated. "One, two, *three!*"

She pushed Jackson forwards, over the gap. Jackson crashed into Lopez's arms. He heaved her across the next stretch of pockmarked tar while Lucy made the leap herself. A metallic groan rang out as the blind colossus stepped on the Humvee, crushing it. The creature staggered towards the bridge.

Lucy grabbed a grenade from her pocket. She yanked the pin out and hurled backward, then sprinted towards the others. The explosion tore through the last passable point of the bridge, severing the creature's path towards them. The blind colossus, screeching and recoiling from the fireball, tumbled sideways into the ravine. The flock of birds dived after it, pouring down into the valley like starlings at night. The creature plunged into the icy water below and thrashed around, screeching, as the torrent swept it away.

Lucy stared at the ruined bridge, panting, and looking forlornly at their crushed vehicle.

"That – was – *horrible*," gasped Maurice.

"You OK?" said Lucy, spotting Jackson, who was bent over, hands on her knees.

"Never better," said Jackson, spitting onto the ground.

"Take cover!" said Lopez.

Lucy whipped around. Two birds were hovering above the broken bridge, facing the group. Two more joined them – ascending from the river. The birds began to advance. In place of beaks they had long, curled tongues which hung from their faces like fine trunks. A fifth bird swooped up from under the bridge and joined them, followed by three more.

"Get to the forest!" Lopez cried.

A whooshing sound swept past Lucy's ears as a needle flew by, embedding itself into the ground with a quiver. It was almost a foot long, and as thick as a porcupine spine.

More spines whooshed through the air. The Canadian sprinted ahead and swiftly disappeared into the trees. The bird's cries became audible – there were no chirps, no squawks, but instead a rasping-hissing sound preceded each attack. Jackson stumbled, dragging Lucy to the ground with her. Lopez scooped under

Jackson's other arm and heaved her upwards. With a cry, the three plunged headfirst into the depths of the forest.

TWO

The

Canadian

A wispy mesh of anemic vines covered the canopy, giving it the appearance of candy floss. As they hurried further inside the forest the snow abated, revealing a carpet of dry leaves. Refracted light rippled across the ground like sunbeams in a swimming pool. Lucy and Lopez dragged Jackson onwards as needles struck the trunks around them.

They covered the length of two football pitches before they caught up with the Canadian, who had stopped beneath a tall, resin-stained tree.

"Stop!" he hissed, turning as the group approached. He held an arm out emphatically, his eyes bulging. With a finger pressed to his lips he pointed to the tall, thin tree behind them. Lucy and Lopez craned their necks awkwardly, hindered by Jackson's weight. In a branch high above them sat a lone bird.

Its black-feathered chest curved outwards, obstructing Lucy's view of its head, but its sharp talons were clear, tightly gripping the spindly branch.

Lopez transferred Jackson's weight onto Lucy and drew his pistol. Silently, he took a dozen steps back from the tree and took aim. Lucy scanned the forest for more birds but the rasping-hissing was gone. The only sound was Lopez's footsteps crunching on the dry leaves, which produced an oddly muffled crinkle.

Lopez moved backwards and circled the tree cautiously, keeping his gun trained on the bird. He stopped at the far side and beckoned Lucy over. She shifted Jackson onto the Canadian, and tip-toed across.

"You ever seen anything like this?" Lopez whispered.

Lucy looked up. The bird's head was missing; its wings and spine had been removed. All that remained was the hollow ribcage, like a vase missing one side. The cavity was filled by a transparent globule the size of a tennis ball, which glistened in the shifting light.

"We need to get away from that right now," said Lucy.

"What is it?" said Lopez.

"Best case scenario, the bird's re-specializing – turning into something else."

"Worst case?"

"Something killed it."

They crept back to the others. Jackson was standing on her own, steadying herself with her hands on her knees, while the Canadian stared nervously at the bird.

"Stay alert, and watch where you step. Canada, you're back man. Young, you're behind Jackson. We go single file, and we go quiet. On me," said Lopez.

***

The forest creaked overhead and rustled underfoot, but the acoustic was ultra-flat; the translucent, tangled ceiling of vines covering the tree tops appeared to muffle all sounds below. Lucy clocked the bird carcass as they passed another resin-stained tree. It was the fourth they'd encountered; hollowed-out and glued to its branch.

They'd walked in silence for what Lucy guessed was a couple of hours, all listening intently for threats and scanning for movement amidst the unending trees. Jackson was growing weak again. Her stumbling gait reminded Lucy of Cassie stumbling around on her birthday. A lifetime ago. Guilt gripped at her chest, tightening the muscles around her ribs like a vice. She had failed to protect the two people closest to her in the world, yet somehow she'd managed to save the three people beside her. The failure made her sick to the core.

Jackson's head was lifted and Lucy followed her gaze. High above the forest floor, skewered by a thick upper branch, hung a parachute. Its chute was torn, and an empty harness dangled below.

The group stopped abruptly. Lopez's hand was raised in a balled fist. Ahead, on the path, lay a long, bent strip of metal.

Lopez signaled them to reform as a horizontal line. They crept forward as one, scouring the debris as they went. Scattered pages from a handbook, bungee cords, and splintered bits of wood littered the forest floor, all leading up to the wreckage of a helicopter.

They moved in. The craft was large – a dark green chinook, heavily damaged. It lay on its side, tilted so far over that it was almost inverted. The cockpit windows were intact, but the seats were empty and the door facing the sky was sealed. The craft's front rotor blades were gone, and the rear of the chopper had been ripped off entirely like a pull-ring can. They skirted its long, scarred, metal body to the back end, which hung open like a broken jaw. The rear propulsion was so twisted and wrenched that it stretched down one side onto the ground like a comb-over.

In the helicopter's wake was a trail of smashed trees. Some were decapitated, others were partially uprooted. Lucy kicked the dry ground leaves aside and revealed the deep impact marks etched into the soil.

"Let's take a look inside. Radio's been torn to pieces but there might be supplies. Jackson, Canada, keep watch. Young, you're with me," said Lopez.

Shafts of light dissected the Chinook, penetrating through the upended, circular cabin windows, the lower halves of which were covered in leaves. Lucy's boots clinked against the metal interior as she followed Lopez inside.

A row of red canvas seats lined each wall, locked in the open position. All were unoccupied. The lower row was covered in broken paneling and insulation which dangled from the roof.

"Check the floor and the overhead compartments for IFAKs, and look for weapons," said Lopez.

Three discarded uniforms lay across the floor. Each had a parachute pack strapped over the sleeves. Lucy put out a hand to balance on the cold metal wall as she stepped between mesh nets and bungee ropes. She kicked over the rubble, searching for something useful amidst the buckled panels and loose cables.

Something glistened beneath a crumpled uniform. Lucy glanced around the cabin. Lopez was interrogating the log book. Lucy drew her gun. She knelt down, staying arm's length from the glistening object, and used the tip of her gun to flick the crumpled sleeve back.

She recoiled with a gasp, swearing loudly.

"Keep it down!" hissed Lopez.

"Sorry, I – look," said Lucy, kicking the rest of uniform aside.

It was a dead fawn. Its legs were lacerated below the knees, and its grey fur was wet. Lucy lifted its head with the tip of her pistol. The fawn's jaw crumpled and bent inwards, releasing drops of Gen Water onto the metal floor like a sponge being wrung out. Lucy tried not to vomit.

"When was it killed?" said Lopez.

"I'd say within the last twenty four hours," said Lucy, swallowing hard.

The deer's head slumped back into place, dragging its body downward, and leaving a white smear on the metal, where the upper body had rested.

"Oh my God," said Lucy, grabbing the carcass and rolling it over. Its legs sheared off, releasing more Gen Water onto the floor, but this time she didn't care, because the freshly-exposed underside was covered in white powder.

"Is that-?" said Lopez.

"Pass my bottle, quick!" said Lucy.

She unfastened the cap and tipped half of the slushy snow water out, then eagerly scooped powder into the flask, coaxing in as much as she could scrape from the foal's coat.

A clinking from the hull interrupted her industry.

"Was that you?" whispered Lucy, looking up.

Lopez's gun was raised. He was staring intently towards the nose of the craft. More clinks. The scrunched curtain by the cockpit rippled.

Lucy silently screwed the cap back onto her bottle and rose to her feet. Lopez wasn't blinking, his eyes fixated on the doorway at the end of the chinook.

"Major?" she breathed.

With a crash, the creature burst out of the cockpit and slithered into the cabin. It was built like a komodo dragon, only its scales were a pattern of scarlet and sunset orange. Its nails rattled against the metal hull as it clawed its way towards them.

"Run!" cried Lopez, firing two rounds at the creature.

"What's going on?" cried Maurice, as Lucy leapt from the wreckage.

"Just go!" cried Lucy, grabbing Jackson by the arm and pulling her forwards. Lopez was close behind, firing backwards as they ran. The canopy swallowed the noise like a silencer.

Lucy raced between the trees until she emerged into a clearing, only to realize the danger too late. She turned and held her finger up to Lopez and the Canadian, who stumbled out after her, spraying snow as they halted.

The tangled translucent vine-ceiling was gone. In the center of the clearing stood a vast tree. Its base was hollowed out, and its lower half showed gnarled stumps where branches used to be. The tree soared above the surrounding canopy, twice the height of the rest of the forest. Birds lined the top branches like leaves. They hadn't yet spotted their prey.

A rock face encircled the clearing, creating a natural amphitheater. A rustling swept towards them like a breaking wave, as the creature sped across the forest floor, camouflaged against the dry leaves.

Lucy redoubled her grip on Jackson and left the forest, making a desperate bid for the far side of the clearing. She glanced back as they passed the towering tree. Only now could she appreciate the size of the pursuing creature. Its length was almost doubled by its thick, armored tail. Its scales flashed red and orange as it weaved towards them. The reptile's strides were uneven; one of its hind legs was withered, its scales bleached yellow-white. But the strength of its other limbs propelled it towards them.

Jackson drowsily raised her rifle but Lucy batted it down.

"No shots – the birds!" Lucy hissed.

"We've gotta climb," urged Lopez, taking Jackson's other arm as they rushed towards the rocky hillside.

Lucy scrambled up onto the first ledge, then pulled Jackson up after her.

"Follow my path," whispered Lucy.

They struggled up the steep rock face, clinging to the sides, hampered by the wet violet moss growing on it. Each ledge was covered in snow, masking the loose rocks which shifted perilously underfoot. As they gained height, the reptile reached the base of the hillside. Lucy's heart froze as she watched the creature hesitate, hindered by its withered leg. Using its thick tail for stability, it clawed its way onto the first ledge.

The group redoubled their escape efforts.

"This way," urged Lucy, picking out a route to the top. She hauled herself up to the next ledge, then reached down for Jackson. Lopez gave Jackson a leg up, while Lucy pulled. Together they heaved her onto the higher tier.

There was a clattering of rocks and a stifled yelp. The Canadian had slipped, and skidded several feet down the slope, towards the oncoming creature. Lopez rushed back down and grabbed him, hauling him back as the creature crawled onto their level. Its scaled feet and sharp nails slapped and scratched against the rock for purchase, as its muscular limbs dragged its diseased leg forwards. A forked tongue stretched before it, trying to reach the two men.

The Canadian scrambled upwards, shoving past Lopez and sending him off balance. Lucy watched in horror as the Major skidded further down the slope towards the creature.

Lopez landed just yards from the advancing reptile. He scrambled to his feet and backed away, missing the upward path and retreating along a ledge which quickly narrowed into nothingness. Tearing off clumps of moss, he clung to the bare rock face as he realized his mistake.

The creature had halted, sniffing. It swiveled around and clambered onto the ledge above, picking up the scent of the Canadian. But Maurice, in his panic, had deviated from Lucy's route, and was struggling to find a way upward.

The reptile closed in. Maurice jumped, grabbing the ledge above. But there were no footholds to be found, and his legs dangled helplessly as he kicked wildly around the smooth rock.

The creature lunged upward at the Canadian. With an almighty wail, Maurice swung his legs out of the way.

"Shit!" cried Lucy, as startled birds fluttered off their branches in droves. A hissing sound filled the air as dozens of black-feathered hunters spotted the new arrivals.

Jackson swung her rifle round and fired six rounds at the creature, but the bullets made little impact on its tough armor.

"Target the leg!" cried Lucy.

Jackson fired on the creature's withered limb. The bullets tore through the bleached scales, causing the reptile to screech in pain and jerk backwards, revealing a softer underbelly. Jackson fired into the creature's exposed underside and the bullets punched through the scales. The creature fell away from the rock face, crashing into the snow below.

"We've got incoming!" cried Lucy, as she reached the summit. She knelt down and pulled Jackson up. The first birds were flying directly towards them. Jackson took up position and fired upon the birds, killing several and dispersing others, while Lucy helped Maurice over the edge. The Canadian staggered to his feet and immediately ran for the cover of the trees, while Lucy waited for Lopez.

She heaved the Major onto the hilltop and the pair ran for the fresh forest, followed by Jackson, who provided covering fire as she ran. With a yell, Jackson emptied her magazine at the birds as the group fled deep into the new forest level. They ran for several minutes until the hissing was no more. Panting, the four regrouped amidst the wispy canopy and dry leaves.

"You're amazing, you're magical, the creature didn't even go near you!" cheered Maurice, panting, and patting Lopez on the back.

Lopez grabbed the Canadian by the throat and pinned him against a tree.

"You shove me down a hillside and think we're all G just because I made it back up alive?" he growled.

"I panicked! I'm sorry!" the Canadian rasped.

"Twice we've saved you, and twice I've asked myself why. Now give me a reason not to *kill* you," said Lopez, his eyes just inches from the other man's.

"Guys, help," said Jackson, from the back.

She was knelt down, head bowed, one hand clutching her flat leg. Sticking out of her calf was a needle.

"Shit," said Lopez, relinquishing his grasp on Maurice, who fell to the ground spluttering.

The top of the needle was fading in color as the oily liquid inside drained into Jackson's leg. Lucy yanked the needle out and tossed it aside, scattering oil and blood among the leaves. Jackson yelled in pain.

"Press down," said Lucy, placing Jackson's hand over the wound. Lucy whipped off her back pack and pulled out a dressing strip, which she wound tightly around Jackson's calf. Then she grabbed her water bottle and unscrewed the cap.

"Drink. It's like Camp Oscar. Do you understand?" said Lucy, thrusting the bottle into Jackson's hand.

Jackson nodded and took a swig of the white powder.

"I could go for some water," said the Canadian.

"Go to hell," said Lopez.

"We need to get moving before the infection takes hold," said Lucy, pulling Jackson to her feet.

"How long does she have?" said Maurice.

"One more word from you and I will end you right here in this forest, you understand?" said Lopez, grabbing his knife and pointing it at Maurice's throat. The man gulped and nodded, hands raised.

"Which way, Major?" said Lucy, re-fastening her backpack.

Lopez consulted his compass and took a bearing.

"East is this way. If you see any creatures, shoot the Canadian first."

**

Welcome to Karen's Mobile Home Park, read the large rusty sign by the side of the highway, and not a moment too soon – Jackson was deteriorating. They'd left the forest some time ago and picked up the highway, having seemingly evaded the birds. But during that time Jackson's complexion had greyed further. She was groggy and swayed as she walked, and looked to be running a fever.

They approached the park entrance – it was the first of four lanes which flowed from the highway like fingers. Each lane hosted a few bungalows of varying size. The row nearest them was bearing the brunt of the snowdrift, which had piled against the rear walls. As they crept through park, Lucy spotted algae growing on the shaded walls between the bungalows. She directed them onto the second row, which looked healthier – a single bungalow with no external growth. Lopez banged on the door and called out several times, but there was no answer.

"I kick, you cover," said Lopez.

Lucy raised her gun. Jackson leaned against the wall, summoning her strength, and also raised her rifle. Lopez kicked the door, hard, breaking the cheap lock and sending it flying open. He sprang back to let Lucy and Jackson cover the entrance. Jackson stumbled forwards, rifle raised. Lucy stayed close behind, as they entered the gloomy abode. Their boots tapped against the vinyl floor as they crossed the short hallway. Lucy's shoulder brushed against the wallpaper; cream with a pattern of lilac buckets. Jackson swung left into the lounge-kitchen area and Lucy followed.

"Clear!" Jackson shouted.

"Clear," came Lopez's reply, from the right hand wing.

He joined them in the lounge.

"Good. This will do. I want a secure base established well before sundown. That gives us thirty minutes, tops. Canada, you're on fuel for a campfire. Jackson, stay here and check for supplies. Young, you and I will do a recce of the other houses for food and water. You take lane three, I'll take four."

"You mean, raid them?" said Lucy.

"Do you have a problem with that?" said Lopez.

"I'd rather not do it alone," Lucy replied, blushing slightly.

"Ditto that. I'll stick with you," said the Canadian.

"There you are, Young, the golden ticket. Don't slow each other down. Clock's ticking people, let's go," said Lopez.

***

Jackson sat slumped on the sofa. She was upright but her eyes were closed, and her ashen cheeks were sagging. Maurice sat across from her, reading a glossy magazine. Lucy was sat on a stool by the fireplace, stirring the pot of simmering pasta. She seized the moment of privacy to capture the tumult of the last two days.

Feb 21st (est.) – I told you about the beast capture mission going wrong, and Rangecroft dying. Well, it turns out Major Lopez blames me, even though it was a joint idea. The fact that we were trying to harvest and grow white powder – the very thing that let Lopez, Jackson, and me escape* – seems to be lost on him. *Escape from Camp Oscar, I mean. The convoy was ambushed, and as far as we know, everyone was killed. The camp had already been attacked – the company we were supposed to rendezvous with had been killed by the time we got there. The creatures had piled up the bodies – presumably to stockpile the Gen Water that would follow. Whatever the impetus, it shows they're capable of complex, goal-oriented tasks.

We're still trying to get to DC to find reinforcements – our truck was destroyed by a colossus, so our progress has been drastically slowed while we're on foot. The colossus was the third of its kind that I've encountered, and it had been blinded by birds. They've evolved projectile needles between their tail feathers. They got Jackson this afternoon. I've given her more white powder but the infection looks terminal. She was only hurt because a stranger made us vulnerable. That's my fault. I thought I was doing the right thing, but now she might die. Another person dying because of me. These people are all I have left. I have to protect them - it can't happen again, I can't be alone again.

Lucy snapped the notebook shut as Lopez's footsteps approached. He was carrying four bowls. He knelt down by Lucy, beside the fireplace, and turned his back on the others.

"How bad is it?" he whispered, checking over his shoulder to be sure Jackson and Maurice weren't listening.

"I don't know. I thought the extra white powder would stabilize the infection, but it's not working," said Lucy.

"What are we talking, days, weeks, hours?"

"Hours," whispered Lucy.

She ladled piping hot pasta from the pot into the bowls Lopez was holding. He passed them to Jackson and Maurice on the sofas, then took a seat as Lucy joined them and passed over his portion. For several minutes the four squatters blew, slurped, and chewed in silence, gobbling the hot food down.

"Man, I could go for some more. That was on *point*," said Maurice, setting his fork down with a clatter.

"You want breakfast tomorrow?" said Lucy.

"Hell yeah!" said the Canadian.

"Then there's no more," she replied.

The Canadian chuckled. "You remind me of my father. He used to say that kinda stuff all the time when I was growing up. He was a real asshole."

"Like father like son," grunted Lucy.

"Am I sensing some hostility?" said Maurice, running his hand through his greying, backcombed hair.

"No hostility, just facts," said Lucy, chewing.

"Wanna tell me about your family? No doubt they were kind-hearted people full of humor," said Maurice.

"Enough of the crap. It's high time you told us who the hell you are, and what you were doing in Cincinnati. Why were you running away from your car?" said Lopez.

"I was out of fuel," shrugged Maurice.

"You were being chased," said Lopez.

"I used up all my fuel trying to get away," said Maurice.

"Away from where?" said Lopez.

"Boston," replied the Canadian.

"Boston?" said Lucy, clattering her fork against the bowl.

"Yeah, good ol' Beantown. Why?" said Maurice.

Lucy's mind flashed to her bedside drawer, back in San Francisco, which contained the life-changing letter. After months of searching, the agency she'd hired had finally tracked her estranged mother down. The woman who'd walked out on her childhood, whom she hadn't seen in years, was living in Boston. With her father long dead, Cassie gone, and Dan's loss achingly raw in her mind, Lucy longed for her mother in a way she hadn't before the disaster. She had become her only living relative.

The thought filled her with longing, anxiety, and hurt all at once. Guilt, too, took hold. She'd never had a chance to tell Dan about the agency's findings. She was going to ask him to come with her, to meet her mom. She'd promised Cassie she'd tell him. Then the satellites failed and everything changed.

"Hello? I said why d'you care about Boston?" said Maurice, snapping his fingers at Lucy.

Lucy blinked sharply and abandoned her ruminations.

"Never mind why she cares, we're interested in what you were doing there," interjected Lopez.

"I was getting the hell out of there," said Maurice.

"Why?" said Lucy.

"Because it's off the chart. You think Cincinnati was bad? Boston's unreal. Apparently there's some doctor trying to fix them, but it's gotta be too late for them. I'm pretty sure they're screwed."

"Who?" pressed Lopez.

"The people. The infected ones," said Maurice, scratching his stubble.

"The virus is still there?"

"Define virus," said Maurice.

"The spores," said Lucy.

"Pff, no – those were months ago. This is way different. Like, zombies different."

"Zombies?" said Lopez, alarmed.

"Not *actual zombies*. No-one's eating brains – those were strictly off the menu. The infected folk just got weak. They'd look like hell for a time, maybe get weird patches on their skin, and then they'd just die."

"They had skin lesions? Are you sure it's a new disease?" said Lucy.

"No idea, didn't stick around to find out," said Maurice.

"And you ended up in Cincinnati?" said Lopez.

"I went via NYC first. Terrible call."

"More of the disease?" said Lucy.

"Nothing like that – not in New York."

"What, then?" pressed Lopez.

"That city's being run by a psychopath. Calls herself 'The Queen'. I got picked up and ended up working for her for a bunch of weeks until I escaped. I was heading for the West Coast when you guys found me."

"There's nothing for you on the West Coast, I promise you that," said Lucy, darkly.

"You guys are from the West?" said the Canadian.

"Lights," interrupted Jackson, pointing outside.

A truck pulled into the mobile park and made a beeline for their bungalow. Lopez grabbed Jackson's rifle and headed for the door. "Young, on me."

The pair of them stepped out into the freezing night. Lucy squinted as the truck approached. Snowflakes danced in the headlights as someone climbed out.

"Who are you?" called Lopez.

The stranger walked closer, into the illumination to reveal a military uniform. He had thin lips, glasses, and bore a sergeant's insignis.

"Five Marines looking for shelter," said the man, assertively.

"Christ you're a sight for sore eyes. Get on in," said Lopez, beckoning them inside.

Five soldiers spilled out of the truck. The driver slung a chain around the steering wheel and locked it in place, before catching up. The soldiers traipsed into the house, not bothering to kick the snow off their shoes. They fell on their knees by the fire and stretched out their hands. The Sergeant – Adler – introduced himself, and the rest of his troop: Willis, Brown, Li, and Peters.

"Told you they was cookin'," said Willis, pointing to the simmering pot. The soldiers' eyes panned hungrily to Lucy and Lopez's brimming plates of pasta. Lucy followed his gaze, which moved from her plate, to her pistol. Her eyes darted to his rifle. She glanced at the other marines. Two more had rifles. All had pistols. The other soldiers' eyes were beginning to wander. Lucy looked at Lopez – he was seeing it too.

"Let's make you and your boys up some pasta, Sergeant, water's still hot," said Lopez.

"Much obliged, Major," said Sergeant Adler.

"Real good of you Major," said the soldier beside him – Willis – who was stroking his thick, unkempt black beard.

"You guys can have the sofa, I'm gonna lie down," said Jackson, shuffling to the edge of the seat.

"Canada, see that our guests are fed. Young, gimme a hand," said Lopez.

Lucy and Lopez helped Jackson down from the sofa onto the floor mattress, while Willis, Peters, and Li all slumped onto the couch.

"What's up with your girl?" said Brown, who had taken the wooden seat by the fire. His lips had a pronounced natural downturn, which gave him a permanent look of depression.

"Fever," said Lucy.

"What kind of fever?" said Brown.

"The kind that makes people sweat," said Lucy.

"Is it contagious?" said the Sergeant, who had remained standing.

"Yes, that's why we're all hanging out together. So we can all catch it," said Lucy, sarcastically.

"No offence, lady, but I ain't sleeping here. I've not made it this far so I can get sick off some stranger," declared Brown, rising from his chair.

"Respectfully, Major, I have to agree with Private Brown here. Brown and I will scout out one of the other houses," said Adler.

"Can us three stay by the fire in the meantime?" asked Li, from the couch. He had a round, child-like face and rosy cheeks to match.

"Fine. But you'll be sharing night watch, so enjoy yourselves while it lasts," said the Sergeant.

Brown tipped his vacant chair over, placed a boot against the frame, and sheared a leg off. He dipped the lower half of the stick into the pot of boiling water then shook it out. He grabbed an empty bowl, threw a tea towel in it, then poured cooking oil over the towel – folding it over several times until it had soaked the load up. He wound the tea towel around the dry end of the chair leg, mopped up the excess oil, then ignited the tip on the fire. Clutching his hand-built torch, he moved towards the doorway.

"Save us some food," said Brown, his face glowing next to the flaming torch.

Sergeant Adler grabbed a rifle and followed after him.

"Your boys seem awful touchy," said Maurice, tipping the last of the dry pasta into the pan.

"They've been through it," said Li, holding his hands out to the fire.

"Well you can relax now. You guys have lucked out big time with this household, take it from me. These two right here – they're special," said the Canadian, pointing towards Lucy and Lopez.

"Special how?" said Li.

"We're really not," said Lucy, anxiously.

"She's just being modest. She saved me from the creatures with her bare hands," said the Canadian.

"You did?" said Li, his eyebrow raised.

"That's not even close to what happened," said Lucy.

"Don't be so modest. There's something about you, like a gift. A lucky charm," said the Canadian.

"We could use some luck," said Li, eyeing her up intently.

"Where'd you say you fellas came from again?" said Lopez.

"All over. Willis is from Detroit, I'm from Atlanta, the Sergeant's from-" began Peters.

"I mean which regiment?" interrupted Lopez.

"Thirty Fourth Infantry," replied Li.

"You're a long way from Minnesota," said Lopez.

"Our division got attacked. We got scattered," Li replied.

"When?" said Lopez.

"About a month ago. We've been trying to get down south – to the coast," said Li.

"Tiny issue of the country's crawling with fuckin' aliens," said Peters. His features were small, and neat, though his lips were chapped.

"It's Armageddon, I been sayin' it for years but none of y'all believed me. We pissed off someone upstairs, and here we are," said Willis.

"Wrong, dumbass. It's the Russians gone done this. They got their labs, doing experiments and shit, and one of their creatures got out and wham, that was it. Now they're all over the world," said Peters. His eyes lit up as he espoused his theory.

"It's not the Russians," said Lucy.

"And you know that how?" said Peters.

"Because it started in space," she replied.

"Bullshit. I don't see no spaceships full of big-assed wolves," snorted Peters.

"It was a bacterial cloud," said Lucy.

"Like, a virus?" said Willis.

"Like a bacteria, moron," said Li.

"The bacteria broke the satellites, then infected some astronauts, who brought it back to Earth," said Lucy.

"Assholes," cried Peters.

"Fuck's sake, Larry, they didn't *mean* to," said Li. "Right?" he added, looking to Lucy.

"Right," said Lucy.

"Hey that kinda figures – we all got given masks right after, cos the disease was in the air," said Willis.

"How'd you explain the wolves, and the bats, and the weird moss stuff on all the buildings?" protested Peters.

"Ever heard the phrase 'you are what you eat?'. That pretty much sums this pathogen up. It kills you, steals your DNA, then does a genetic lottery when it respawns. It's how it's scaled up," said Lucy.

"Respawns?" said Li.

"They don't breed like we do. D4 creatures are self-replicating. They don't need the genetic variance of two parents, because they get it from their prey. But their mechanism is insane – it's a reversal of what happens in human wombs. Every cell in the creature's body reverts to a base state, so that you're effectively left with a ball of stem cells, which then turn into something based on stolen DNA."

"But if there's no parent, how come you got whole packs of wolves?" said Peters.

"I'm guessing there's some kind of horizontal gene transfer at play. Like in bacteria, which share successful adaptations – they could be sharing entire genetic maps. Maybe they infect each other with those maps, in the same way they infect their prey with some kind of enzyme. But that's the crazy thing – here you've got a single pathogen taking a huge number of forms and competing against itself."

"She gonna eat that?" said Willis, pointing to Jackson's half-eaten plate of pasta.

"Maybe in the morning," said Lucy.

"Huh," grunted the soldier, scratching his bushy cheek.

"How often do the creatures respawn?" said Li.

"We actually don't know what prompts the respawning, but the rate seems to correlate to size. Bigger variants take longer to breed, and will need more food, so you'll see fewer of them. Plus they may be outcompeted by smaller ones," said Lucy.

"How'd you know all that?" said Peters, eyeing her up suspiciously.

"She's a scientist," said Lopez.

"My colleagues figured it out, actually," said Lucy.

"Where are they now?" said Willis.

Lucy stared at the fire.

"What kind of question is that?" hissed Li.

"I'm just asking, maybe they in a bunker or somethin'?" muttered Willis.

"They're dead," said Lucy, loudly.

"A'ight, so now we know. No bunker," said Willis, shrugging.

"You said it is what it eats. You reckon that explains the zombie people?" asked Peters.

"They're not 'zombies', man. They don't eat brains, or bite people," said Li.

"They look like shit and everyone avoids them, they might as well be," said Peters.

"That sounds more like leprosy," said Lucy.

"I heard Boston's crawling with 'em," said Willis.

"I've heard your rumors before, and you boys ain't seen shit to prove it," said Li.

"I have," said Maurice.

All eyes fell on the Canadian.

"I've seen them. They're definitely *not* zombies, by the way," Maurice added, passing around bowls full of hot pasta, which the soldiers devoured ravenously.

"But those people are sick, right? Like, alien sick?" said Peters, chomping away.

"Yeah, they're pretty messed up. No-one knows what it is, but it's spreading" said Maurice.

"D'you find *her* in Boston?" said Willis, nodding at Jackson.

"She drank some bad water is all. Be glad she's stopped shitting everywhere," said Lucy.

"If one of you starts shitting everywhere, I will one hundred percent leave you to die in it. Just sayin'," said Willis, prompting Li and Peters to laugh.

"All of them die anyway," said Maurice.

"I heard they found a cure – some doctor lady?" said Peters.

"You can just say 'doctor'," said Lucy.

"So she's real?" said Li.

Maurice shrugged.

Jackson spluttered from the mattress, muttered some incoherent words and rolled onto her side.

"Yo, you got any more?" said Willis.

"How are you finished already?" said Li.

"I'm done too," said Peters.

"You two are animals," said Li.

"That's it, I'm afraid," said Maurice, collecting up the bowls.

"Fuck it, I'm having hers," said Willis, reaching for Jackson's portion.

Lucy leapt up and kicked Willis's hand away.

"That's hers," said Lucy, sharply, scooping the bowl up from the floor.

"The fuck?" said the soldier, leaping to his feet. He lashed out and struck the bowl from Lucy's hands. It fell to the floor and smashed, sending shards of porcelain and pasta across the vinyl.

"The hell are you doing?" cried Lopez, leaping to his feet.

"Bitch just kicked me!" yelled Willis.

"Woah, easy there, let's all keep it friendly," said Maurice, raising his hands.

"I'll be calm when I've kicked this bitch back," fumed Willis.

"You're not hearing me, soldier. I said *take a seat*," said Lopez.

"Or what?" said Willis, squaring up to the Major.

"You don't like our hospitality, you're welcome to leave," growled Lopez.

"I'm liking it just fine," said Willis.

Lopez's hand edged towards his pistol.

"Try it," Willis grunted.

The front door clattered open. Sergeant Adler and Private Brown appeared in the threshold.

"The hell's going on here?" said Adler, seeing Lopez and Willis standing across from one another, each with a hand on their holster.

"It's nothing, just a misunderstanding. We're all good," said Peters, rising from the couch and patting Willis on the back. Willis didn't move.

"We've set up the house across the yard. Fire's going," said Adler.

"We'll be turning in, then. Come on boys," said Peters, steering Willis towards the door.

"We're gonna keep a night watch. You guys want in? We rotate every two hours," said the Sergeant.

"We'll do our bit, of course. Who goes first?" said Lopez, smoothing his uniform.

"I could take first shift – I do owe you guys," said Maurice, shrugging.

"Yes, you do," said Lopez.

"Does he know what he's doing?" said Adler.

"He knows how to cry for help loudly," said Lopez.

"I guess that'll do," said the Sergeant, departing, followed by the other soldiers.

"I get a gun, right? I'd feel a lot more comfortable if I had a gun," said Maurice.

"I'll make a note of that for next time," said Lopez.

The Canadian let out a nervous laugh and lingered a moment. Then, realizing the gun was not forthcoming, he headed outside, cursing.

Lopez grabbed a dustpan and brush and swept up the shattered porcelain, while Lucy gathered the pieces of pasta into a new bowl. Once it was cleared, the pair headed to the bedroom to retrieve the second mattress and move it into the warm room. A glow outside caught Lucy's eye.

"You see that?" she said, pointing outside.

Three cigarettes glimmered in the darkness.

"Grab the goggles," said Lopez.

Lucy fetched the night vision from her back pack and handed them to Lopez.

"What do you see?" she asked.

"Maurice – that asshole's smoking with two of them," said Lopez.

"Which two?" said Lucy.

"The Sergeant and your new best friend, Willis. Hold on, they're going inside," said Lopez.

"I thought he was on watch?"

"This isn't right. I don't trust any of them – none of their stories hang together, and that Canadian's a piece of shit," said Lopez.

"You think they're gonna attack us?"

"I don't know. They know we're outnumbered, and outgunned But they know the blood rule, surely? What would they gain from killing us?" said Lopez.

"What if killing's not the aim?" said Lucy.

"So what, they just wanna take us prisoner?"

"You heard Maurice back there, he's figured it out. He knows we're immune to the creatures, and the soldiers know we're heading to DC but they want to go south. What if they want to capture us for safe passage?" said Lucy.

Lopez peered through the window again.

"Get down!" he hissed, hitting the deck.

Lucy copied.

"They're moving on us. Two left, two center, two right. We need to get to the forest. On me," said Lopez, running through to the lounge room.

"Hostiles incoming, we gotta move quiet and fast," said Lopez, rousing Jackson.

Jackson, staggered to her feet and grabbed her rifle while Lucy grabbed her backpack.

"Get to the next house. Get behind it, then move to the end of the row. Then run for the trees," ordered Lopez.

He clicked the rear door open and hurried them out, sealing it behind as he followed.

The snow glowed as if under a UV light. Their footsteps crunched as they rushed to the next house. Lucy sped around the corner and sprinted to the end of the row, pushing out wide to avoid the snowdrifts. She reached the last house and halted. The forest was at last a hundred yards away. Jackson was lagging behind – aided by Lopez, who was supporting most of her weight. Lucy ran back and took Jackson's other arm. A crash came from their deserted bungalow as the rear door was kicked open.

"Hurry!" whispered Lopez, as they dragged Jackson forwards. Jackson pulled her arms in and fell to her knees as they reached the end house.

"What are you doing?" urged Lucy.

Jackson swung her rifle into position and took the safety off.

"Covering you. Now go."

"You heard her, *go!*" said Lopez, shoving Lucy forwards.

She sprinted towards the forest, past an abandoned car. Lopez drew level beside her. A whistle blasted. Shots rang out as Jackson opened fire, silencing the scout. An engine roared into life and the soldier's truck sped towards the gunfire.

Lucy glanced back as she ran, terrified. The truck swung out onto the final lane. Jackson took up position behind the abandoned car and fired upon the Hummer, but couldn't penetrate the windshield.

With a crunch, the Hummer shunted her covering place. Jackson jumped but the car clipped her legs, knocking her to the ground.

Lucy sprinted into the dark forest.

"This way!" called Lopez, changing direction from the trail of footprints they'd left in the field.

"We got your girl," came a shout from the yard.

Lucy and Lopez stopped abruptly, panting. They peered back between the slender trees. The Humvee's lights shone across Jackson's crumpled body. Looming over her was Adler. The Sergeant grabbed her by the hair and hauled her onto her knees. Her right leg was broken, and swiveled outwards perpendicular to its normal positon. Jackson screamed in pain.

"I'm gonna give you fuckers till the count of five to surrender," yelled Adler, looking around the treeline.

"Either we surrender now or we keep running. She can't suffer for nothing," whispered Lucy, to Lopez.

"In fact, your girl's gonna help me do the counting," yelled the Sergeant. "Here goes. One!"

He snapped Jackson's index finger back, splitting the bone, and extorting a guttural howl from her.

Lopez drew his handgun and took aim. Lucy covered her ears.

"Two!" cried Adler.

Lopez fired. The bullet ripped through the side of Jackson's head and her body went limp, slumping to the ground.

"Run!" cried Lopez, as Adler leaped into the Humvee.

The truck raced towards the forest, heading in the direction of the gunshot. Its lights cut through the thin trees like trip wires. Lucy and Lopez sprinted further into the forest, dodging the solid trunks as they ran, trying to escape the lights. But as the Humvee reached the forest edge the lights went dead. Lucy suddenly stopped, finding herself in total darkness.

"Young, keep moving!" called Lopez, in a coarse whisper.

She hurried towards his voice, ricocheting off invisible trunks.

"Major!" she whispered, trying to keep up.

The reply was imperceptible.

"*Major!*" she implored.

Silence.

Lucy came to a halt and an icy chill swept over her. The snow had gone. Twigs and leaves crackled in all directions.

"*Hurry!*" came a whisper.

She rushed towards the sound.

"Come on!"

She stumbled onward, desperately feeling her way.

"Young!"

She tacked to her left, struggling to keep pace with the zigzagging voice.

"Young, come on!" urged the voice, from the other direction.

She stopped.

"Quickly!"

The whispering was on both sides.

"This way!"

It was closing in.

"*Hurry!*"

"Lucy, no!"

A blow from the side. Someone tackled her to the ground with immense force. She landed hard on her shoulder, tightly bound by the stranger's arms. Lucy squirmed as the assailant wrestled her onto her front. Leaves and dirt rubbed against her face. The soldier straddled her back, pinning her down with his weight, and stifling her breaths.

"I got the girl!" cried Peters, pinning her.

"Major, it's time to give up. Accept that you've lost, and we can avoid further tragedy!" called Adler, somewhere ahead of Lucy.

"In case you're thinking of shooting one of us, I promise you we'll shoot your girlfriend right away, and we really don't wanna do that – not after all this," the Sergeant continued. "We don't wanna shoot you at all. Word on the street is that you two are quite the catch. But it's all or nothing now, Major. Either both of you get to live, and we settle this like adults, or we'll kill her right here, right now. Then after that, we'll find you, and we'll kill you too. I'm a man of my word, sir, so I really suggest you go for the first option."

"Just listen to him, Major, it didn't have to go like this," called Maurice.

Lucy's blood boiled.

"Freeze!" cried Brown, somewhere in the darkness. "Drop your weapon. Get down on the ground, hands behind your back!"

"Good choice, Major. Alright team, let's get back," cheered Adler.

Peters patted Lucy on the back. "Sweet dreams," he chuckled, before delivering a sharp crack to the back of her head.

THREE

Citizens

"The principal will see you now, my dear," said the receptionist. Lucy thanked him awkwardly, unsure why the world's surliest front-desker was suddenly being nice – especially when she'd been summoned out of her math class. Maybe it was a trick. He probably knew what kind of telling off she was in store for.

The principal opened the door and beckoned Lucy inside. The portly woman was wearing her usual teal cardigan and white blouse combo.

"Lucy, great to see you. Come on in," said the principal.

Lucy spotted the school counsellor sitting by the sofas.

"Please, take a couch," said the principal, taking one herself.

Lucy sat down on the sofa opposite. The fibers were a little scratchy, but the padding was soft. She shuffled towards one side of the three-seater.

"Lucy, I've got some bad news. There's no easy way to say this, but I want you to know we're all here for you," said the counsellor.

Lucy looked blankly from the counsellor to the principal, both of whom wore the same, pitying smiles.

"What's going on?" said Lucy.

"Your father's been taken to hospital," said the counsellor.

"What?" said Lucy, immediately standing up.

"Please sit back down for a moment, Lucy. You'll get to see him shortly but we need to talk things through first," said the principal.

Lucy sat, but her mind was spinning, already rushing through the route to the hospital, picturing her father in a stretcher, wrapped in plaster after an awful traffic incident.

"Your father is sick, Lucy. He's got advanced cancer. It's amazing they've caught it in time – any longer and, well, it really is a good thing they found it when they did."

"Is he going to die?" said Lucy.

"They've got some great doctors working on his treatment plan as we speak," said the counsellor.

"Lucy, we couldn't get hold of your mother, do you know if she's changed her phone number or email?" said the principal.

Lucy stared at her feet.

"It's OK if you don't know – I just wanted to check you hadn't heard from her," said the principal.

"Not in two years," said Lucy, kicking her heels together.

"OK sweetie. Look, your father's going to be in hospital for a few days while they run some tests and he's asked Emily's parents to look after you until he's back."

"Emily's parents? Have you *met* Emily's parents? They're Flat Earthers! She can't stay with Emily, she'll go insane!" protested Dan, leaping up.

Lucy yanked him back down onto the sofa next to her.

"Shut up, you'll get us in trouble," hissed Lucy, blushing and giggling.

"I'm saying it how it is. Screw Emily's parents. Come on," said Dan, grabbing Lucy's hand and pulling her from the room. The receptionist rose to his feet in astonishment as the pair flew by, ignoring his waving clipboard.

"Where are we going?" said Lucy, breathlessly, as they ran down the school steps into the parking lot, basking in the afternoon sun.

"To your mom's," said Dan, putting on his sunglasses.

"You don't even know where she lives," giggled Lucy, as she followed him to their car.

"Sure I do," said Dan, waving a folded letter in his hand.

They reached a small Chevy hatchback and Dan pulled the driver's door open and climbed inside. Lucy stopped suddenly.

"What is it?" said Dan, poking his head over the door.

"This isn't our car," said Lucy.

"Clock's ticking, honey, don't flake on me now. We need to get the rations to your mom's by nightfall," said Dan.

Lucy felt hot. Her hazmat suit was baking in the sun. Dan slammed the door and reversed.

"Wait, for me!" she cried, pedaling to no avail as her bike wheels spun out on the slushy carpet of spores.

***

Lucy opened her eyes to find a boot close to her nose. Her cheek was pressed against the truck's corrugated metal floor, which carried the engine's vibrations. Wet fibers pushed against her tongue. She was gagged. Her hands and feet were bound tightly, too. She craned her neck and took in the rest of the truck. Willis and Peters sat on one bench, Brown on another. Lopez was sat on the floor, his back propped up against the foot of the bench. He was similarly bound and gagged, but also had a ripening black eye. He looked balmy.

"Look who's up," said Peters, toasting her with his water bottle.

Willis grunted and gave Lucy a cold look. Brown stared into the distance.

Lucy wriggled herself towards the wall opposite Lopez and, with difficulty, squirmed into an upright position. Her head swam, and the bruise on the back of her skull throbbed painfully. Her arms ached from being pinned behind her back. The truck had an open back, like the carriers she been loaded into for the evac train months ago. Behind them was an expanse of snow-covered farmland. Theirs were the only tread marks on the highway.

She tried to loosen the bindings around her wrists, but they were solid. She shouted through the gag, as best she could, but the soldiers ignored her. So she banged her boots against the metal floor until Peters intervened.

"*What?*" he said, pulling the gag down roughly.

"Where are you taking us?" croaked Lucy, her throat dry.

"Shut your mouth," said Peters, moving to replace the gag.

"Wait – I need to pee," said Lucy.

"Then pee," said Peters.

"Water!" cried Lucy.

Peters grabbed his bottle and held it to Lucy's mouth. Water trickled down her chin as the truck jostled, but she got a few precious sips before Peters snatched the bottle away again, and jerked her gag back into place.

The truck slowed to a halt. Four thumps came through from the driver's cabin.

"If you want to live, you'll both stay quiet. If I hear any noise, I'll kill whoever makes it. We only need one of you to get there alive," said Willis. He grabbed Lucy by the shoulders and dragged her down

71

to the floor, doing the same to Lopez, before covering them both with a blanket.

The truck came to a halt. Lucy strained to listen through the stifling polyester. The driver was talking to someone in another truck. The only words she caught from the strangers were 'Senator' and 'nightfall'. Sergeant Adler replied from their cockpit, and his words sent a chill down Lucy's spine.

"We're transporting two deserters to DC for court martial. They killed one of our men. We rescued this civilian along the way," said Adler.

The Canadian greeted the other driver.

"I hope you find the Senator, Lieutenant," said Adler.

The two trucks pulled away from one another. Several minutes passed before the blanket was pulled off, and Lucy and Lopez were left to struggle back into their upright positions.

Over the next couple of the hours the snowy farmland view gave way to urban sprawl. They crossed two bridges, passing through Staten Island and into Brooklyn, where the truck slowed. They slalomed between burned out cars which had been deliberately arranged to slow any approaching vehicle. Shortly after, the truck came to a stop and after a moment the engine cut out. Adler and the Canadian walked around to the rear of the truck.

"We did the flashes but they're not opening the gate. I guess they changed the passcode or whatever. We're going through on foot," said Maurice.

Willis and Brown dragged Lucy and Lopez from the truck. Peters cut the ties around their ankles, then marched them to the front of the vehicle. Three buses were parked across the street, wall to wall, blocking the entire way through. As they got closer, it became apparent they were arranged like bricks – with a narrow gap between the overlapping areas.

"Wait here, I'll go announce us, then you guys come through," said Maurice. He squeezed between the buses and disappeared. "Did you miss me?" he called out from the other side, to an unknown audience. His voice echoed off the surrounding buildings.

"Disarm your group, deposit their weapons, then tell them to come through one at a time," ordered the stranger. Her laconic voice crackled through the loudhailer.

The Canadian squeezed back through between the buses.

"They want you to hand over your weapons first," he said, peering around the gap.

"Yeah, we heard," said Adler.

"You didn't say nothin' about disarming," said Brown, his nostrils flaring.

"You'll get your weapons back, it's just a precaution," insisted Maurice, raking his dark backcomb with his fingertips.

"To hell with that," said Willis, spitting on the ground, then wiping the residual spittle from his wiry black beard.

"If you don't like it, you can piss off back to whatever shitty little wilderness you came from. I'm sure the facilities are excellent there," crackled the loudhailer lady.

Willis spun around, his rifle raised, his eyes darting across the surrounding buildings.

"If you've got any sense, you'll suck it up, hand over your weapons, and come get a new life," she added. Her voice was droll, blurring the line between bored and playful.

"Rifles only," ordered Adler, concealing his pistol. Peters, Willis, and Brown followed suit, before placing their rifles around Maurice's neck – each eyeballing him angrily as they did so.

The Canadian slipped back through between the buses, clattering the guns against them as he went, before loudly and piously depositing them in the open.

"Come through, one at a time, with your hands raised," ordered the loudhailer lady.

"God dammit," said Adler, disappearing between the buses.

Peters went next, with one arm chaperoning Lopez behind him. Brown went next and similarly pulled Lucy through. Willis followed close behind.

Lucy squeezed around between the buses and emerged onto the other side of the street. The soldiers had their arms raised. Lucy copied Lopez's tactic and turned side-on to the building to show that her hands were tied behind her back.

"None of you move," ordered the loudhailer lady.

They stood at the end of the street, which formed a T-junction, headed up by a large office building backing onto the waterfront. Behind it was the sea, and a bridge leading to Manhattan. Before them was wall-to-wall razor wire. The road to the left was similarly blockaded by trucks and cars. The blockade to the right was further down the street, at the far end of the waterfront building. If this place was anything like her co-working space in San Francisco, there could easily be room for a couple of hundred companies in there.

A gaunt young man of around twenty emerged from the front door of the office, clutching an empty cloth bag. He approached the left wall of the street. Between the razor wire and the brick was a metal sheet, fixed to the wall. At the base was a jack, which he cranked several times. As the base of the sheet pivoted away from the wall, it pushed the razor wire back, creating a wedge shaped opening.

The skeletal man crawled through the gap in the razor fence and approached Maurice. He patted him down then moved on to Adler and the rest of the group. He removed each soldier's pistol and grenades, which he placed into the cloth bag. He checked Lucy's backpack and moved on, satisfied it was clean. The man scooped up the four rifles and swung them over his neck, then crawled back through the wedge gap and returned to the office building.

"You may enter. Come through the fence, nice and slow," ordered the loudhailer lady.

Cursing, the soldiers got onto their hands and knees and followed Maurice through the wedge. Lopez hesitated, kneeling, unable to crawl without his arms. Brown reached through and dragged Lopez by the shoulders, then reach in and grabbed Lucy, dragging her through too. It would've shredded her knees were it not for the layer of snow.

"Don't be shy," crowed the loudhailer lady.

"Let me do the speaking guys, just trust me. You don't wanna say the wrong thing," said Maurice, as they approached.

The building had a spacious, high-ceilinged atrium and a yuppie-industrial aesthetic. Redundant filament bulbs dangled in trendy cages, complementing the tastefully-rusted metalwork and exposed trunking, which were offset against the dark polished stone counters.

A woman of Lucy's age stood waiting for them. She had light ginger hair, pale skin, hoop earrings, and a face covered in blotchy brown freckles. She was flanked by two guards.

"Marissa, fantastic to see you again," said Maurice, with a slight squawk.

Marissa said nothing, and continued chewing her gum, while staring at the Canadian.

"I've brought a gift for the Queen. Two, actually," Maurice added nervously, gesturing to Lucy and Lopez.

"We're full," said Marissa.

"She's gonna want to meet these two, trust me," said Maurice.

"I bet you my dinner the boss kills him outright," said Marissa, turning to a guard, who snorted and declined the wager as a fait accompli.

"I'm confident the Queen will welcome these new assets," Maurice insisted, with a pained smile.

"Guess we'll find out. Come on then," said Marissa.

They climbed the window-lit stairwell for several minutes in silence, save for the group's puffing and panting. Lucy's bound hands put a strain on her shoulders and chest, making the climb harder still. The sensation reminded her of the climbs she and Dan had made to their eighth-floor apartment, carrying rations, wearing hazmat suits, moving bodies. As she thought of his face, his voice, his counsel, a knot formed in the pit of her stomach.

Lucy arrived at the ninth floor feeling light-headed. Marissa delivered several knocks on the door in a distinctive pattern. A key turned and the threshold swung opened, revealing a perfectly-lit corridor. Bright, recessed ceiling lights shone down on thick, emerald carpet and black wooden doors. Music reverberated from one of the furthest apartments.

The guard waved Marissa in, then stopped the Canadian. "Arms out," he ordered.

"Is this really necessary?" sighed Maurice, raising his arms.

The guard patted him down thoroughly, then allowed him to join Marissa in the corridor. He moved on to the soldiers, screening and admitting them one by one.

"I'm getting tired of this bullshit. Pay off better be worth it, Canada man, or you'll be paying," said Willis, as the guard felt down each of his legs.

Once the guard had finished with the three soldiers, and Lucy, and Lopez, he waved Marissa's guards through, before locking the door behind them all.

Marissa led the way to the furthest apartment. She delivered another coded knock but it was lost against the blaring music. She tried again, then pounded the door with her palm until a guard let them in.

The room was a penthouse suite, decorated with white leather sofas, faux fur carpets, and a chandelier. A nervous-looking father and young daughter sat on the nearest sofas. The father wore a sleeveless body-warmer over a grubby jumper. His limited hair sat around his head like a wreath that had slipped. His daughter wore a banana-yellow tracksuit, and had her fingers pressed into her ears. Next to her was a furry rainbow pencil case. On the sofa opposite sat two guards, dressed in black, both armed with Tasers.

A DJ stood at the far end of the room, hunched over a double turntable. He bopped along, fussing over the faders and dials with real panache, making no perceptible difference to the sound but looking busy nonetheless.

Over by the far window stood a large desk. Behind it sat a large, besuited woman in her late fifties, who was filling out paperwork while gently nodding along to the expletive-riddled beats. She had dark brown skin and thick, frizzy black hair embellished with bronze highlights. She wore skinny jeans, a white blouse, and a navy blue blazer. Lucy assumed this to be 'the Queen'. Marissa led the group forwards, and announced their presence loudly over the blaring music. The Queen ignored them. Marissa signaled the DJ to dull slash the volume, which he did, and she repeated her announcement.

"Did I tell you to turn the volume down?" said the Queen, not bothering to look at the DJ directly but continuing to write instead.

"Ma'am, your guests were-" stammered the DJ, but the Queen silenced him with a finger. She took another minute to finish writing, then placed her pen down and looked up, past the new arrivals, to the sofa. She beckoned the young girl over to the desk. "Can you read, honey?"

"Yeah," said the girl.

"Good. Read this out so your daddy can hear," said the Queen.

"You fucking kidding me?" mumbled Willis, earning him an elbow in the ribs from Adler.

The girl stumbled through the contract aloud.

"I, Reginald Barrow, agree to the following terms in return for life-preserving medication for my daughter Cynthia. Cynthia Barrow will assist in laundry and textile services for eight weeks from the commencement of this contract. During this period I will forgo my usual privileges and will report to the Clinician, whom I will assist in his service to the Queen. I agree to undertake all and any duties required by him to fulfil my debt."

Marissa shared a wince with her nearest guard.

"Beautifully read," said the Queen, patting the girl on the shoulder. "Now take this to your daddy, with this pen. All he needs to do is sign it, then you can get a brand new inhaler right away."

The child grinned and skipped back to her father, who received the paperwork with a tremble.

"The Clinician," he stammered, looking imploringly to the Queen.

"If the terms are too much for your daughter, there's no obligation to sign, Reginald. You're free to walk away," said the Queen, sitting back in her chair with her hands clasped.

The man looked at his daughter and his face fell. He signed the document, then dropped the pen on the coffee table.

"Take that to level five for stamping and they'll take it from there," said the Queen.

"Thank you!" cheered the young girl, as she pulled her dad towards the exit, excitedly.

"Bye sweetie," waved the Queen.

The Queen approached the side counter where she took a jug of filter water and used it to top up a kettle, which she flicked on. She took a mug and saucer from the side and laid them out, placing a black teabag inside with the tag draped over the rim. As the kettle gently boiled, she strolled to the window and gazed across the water to Lower Manhattan. Willis let out a series of increasingly conspicuous huffs until, after a minute of being silently ignored, he could contain his impatience no longer.

"Yo, lady, you want what we sellin' or not? We come a long-assed way to-" he began.

The Queen interrupted him with a raised hand.

Willis regrouped and continued, more aggressively. "You fucking for real? You basically strip search us out in the damned snow, then make us stand around while you do some weird hip-hop poetry ritual or whatever that was. Naw, I'm callin' it – we here to sell or we leavin'. So are you here to buy or what?"

The Queen sighed, and continued looking across the water.

"It's always such a pity," she said, wistfully.

"What's 'a pity'?" sneered Willis.

"You have high hopes for someone, then you discover they're not a quick learner. Marissa, tell me, is it proper to speak to one's leader without being invited?"

"No, ma'am, it's disrespectful," said Marissa.

"Indeed. And what is a leader without respect?"

Marissa hesitated.

"It's not a trick, honey. I know you know the answer," added the Queen.

"They're nothing?" said Marissa.

"Precisely. Which puts me in a difficult situation, does it not? Either I accept that the newcomer does not respect me, and in doing so condone the erosion of my own leadership, *or* I gain his respect, and the balance is restored."

The kettle climaxed to a boil and clicked off.

"Guys, would you mind?" said the Queen, addressing Marissa's guards with a modest smile.

The pair seized Willis's arms from behind. One kicked his knee, sending him to the ground, while the other twisted Willis's wrist backward, forcing him to cry out. Before the other soldiers could intervene, the guards on the sofa leapt up and trained their Tasers on the group – as did Marissa and the DJ.

The guards forced Willis over to the kettle. They grabbed his spare hand and slammed it over the spout. Willis yelped in pain as the searing metal scolded his skin. Marissa waltzed over and turned the kettle back on, keeping her finger depressed on the switch. The kettle boiled furiously, spewing steam into Willis's palm. The soldier screamed in agony and begged for it to end.

After eight agonizing seconds, the Queen called them off. The soldiers released Willis and he fell to the ground, clutching his hand, sobbing. Gasping for breath, and trying to stifle his sobs with grunts, he rose to his knees and staggered back towards the group. His cheeks were wet, and mucus streamed from his nose. He fell in line behind Brown and Peters, next to Lucy, with his head bowed.

The Queen returned to the kettle and poured herself a cup of tea. She peeled open a packet of UHT soya milk and tipped it in, then stirred.

"I've gotta hand it to my team. I don't know *where* they keep finding these sachets. I swear I drank Brooklyn dry months ago," said the Queen.

"There's still Manhattan and Queens," chipped Marissa.

"That *is* good news. Marissa, honey, a question for you. A radio's gone missing from the textiles floor. How shall we get it back?" said the Queen.

"Address the whole floor, tell them what's happened and give them a deadline to find and return it?" suggested Marissa.

"What if they miss the deadline?" said the Queen.

"Then no-one on that floor eats until it's returned," Marissa shrugged.

"Is that the best way?" said the Queen.

"I guess it could piss people off," Marissa conceded.

"Why should that matter to us?" pressed the Queen.

"Because most of those people are loyal?" said Marissa.

"Do they deserve to be punished for someone else's error?" said the Queen.

"No, ma'am," frowned Marissa.

"So perhaps an alternative?" said the Queen.

"We could talk to some of them in private – the reliables. Quietly find out who did it then punish them publicly?"

"Why is that better?"

"Keeps people on side and sends a message. Could deter other people from doing the same thing?" said Marissa.

"You'd better get started. Talk of the theft will already be spreading. Let's turn that into talk of the consequences. Oh, and take mister beardy big mouth here down to medical as you go – the first ten minutes are so important for burns," added the Queen, gesturing to Willis, who remained hunched over in pain.

"What about the others?" said Marissa, nodding at the group.

"I'll deal with them," said the Queen.

Marissa bowed and took Willis from the room.

The Queen added two spoonfuls of sugar to her tea and stirred it, before clinking the spoon noisily against the sides, setting the spoon down on the counter, and addressing the group. "I'm developing her management skills. I've always felt a personal obligation to nurture potential wherever I find it. Marissa's weakness is that she's too keen to impress me. It makes her reach for heavy-handed solutions, and they can cause more problems than they solve, you know? But Marissa's hard-working and she's loyal. If you're both of those things, you'll thrive here. Which brings me to you, Maurice, does it not? No doubt you'll tell me you worked hard to get back here, but I think we can agree there's a question mark over your loyalty," said the Queen.

She blew across the hot cup then stared at Maurice while taking a sip.

"Well? Out with it," she prompted.

Maurice edged forwards, wary of the Tasers still being levied at him. He fell to his knees, clasped his hands, and looked up at the Queen. "My Queen, I was a fool to leave you. I planned to return and tell you I was, like, *super* sorry, but after everything you've done for me, I knew I needed more than an apology. So I scoured the nation until I found a gift worthy of you, and yesterday I found them. The first humans who are immune to those *horrible* alien beasts," said Maurice, rising to his feet and gesturing to Lucy and Lopez with a bow.

"Immune how?" said the Queen, eyeing Lucy up as the Canadian presented her and Lopez.

"The creatures are scared of them, ma'am. I've seen it. They won't attack them, or even touch them. It's incredible, they're like human shields," said the Canadian, circling Lucy like she was a collectible.

"That's quite a claim," said the Queen, taking another sip of tea.

"I've seen it in action. I was being attacked by a beast and the woman put herself between me and it. The way the creature backed out – it was like she was on fire or something. Then him, this guy, he's unreal. The Major fell down a rock face, right into this reptile creature's path, and the thing backed away. It went *around* him," said Maurice, framing Lopez with his hands.

The Queen said nothing and continued sipping her tea. Maurice cleared his throat and continued, nervously. "The woman, she's a scientist, too," he said, opening Lucy's backpack and pulling out the green paste. "She put this stuff on my hand when I got cut. It stopped the bleeding and covered up the scent so the creatures didn't detect us."

He passed the tub to the Queen, who inspected it.

"Ungag her," the Queen ordered.

A guard removed Lucy's gag.

"What is this?" said the Queen, waving the tub at Lucy.

"I don't know. My predecessor made it. But it works like he said," said Lucy, nodding at Maurice.

"Bring me whatever else she's got in there," said the Queen, gesturing to Lucy's backpack. A guard pulled out Lucy and Rangecroft's notebooks and handed them over.

"These yours, too?" said the Queen, flicking through both.

"One is," said Lucy.

"I see. You can go now. I'll call for you when I'm ready," said the Queen, taking a seat at her desk and opening Lucy's diary. She snapped her fingers and the DJ cranked the volume as the guards chaperoned the group out into the hall.

Lucy took care not to overbalance as they descended the staircase, her stability hampered by her tied hands. A few floors down, Brown, Adler, and Peters were separated from Lucy and Lopez and taken away onto that level. Lucy and Lopez were escorted down two more floors then shown into a level filled with glass office cubicles. The guard slid a nearby cubicle open and moved Lucy inside, but blocked Lopez, who was still gagged, from entering. The guard cut the cords binding Lucy's hands, then slid the glass door shut and locked her inside.

Lopez was led away around the corner and out of sight. Lucy glanced around the rest of the floor. The other cubicles were filled with people of different ages, laboring. Some were stripping electrical cables, others were stuffing rags into cushions, others were charting a route across a map of the city. She re-examined her own cubicle. It was around five yards wide, and eight yards long. Wooden desks lined each glass wall in a U-shape. Upon them sat Macs and keyboards, and various charging ports. In the corner was a bucket of water, a sponge, and an empty bucket. In the middle of the floor, a makeshift bed of sofa cushions and a sleeping bag had been laid out. Next to it lay a towel and fresh night clothes.

The office had no blinds, but the lower half of the glass was frosted, so Lucy knelt down and stripped off. She gave herself a brisk clean with the cold water, wincing as she pressed the tender, bruised parts of her shoulder where Peters had tackled her in the forest. Below the bruising she noticed blotches on her upper arm. She checked the other arm – they were there too. The skin looked dry and irritated, and had a reddish tinge. She dried herself off, changed into the night clothes, and crawled into the sleeping bag. As she closed her bloodshot eyes, she couldn't help but picture Jackson's crumpled body. She had been kind to Lucy, in the end. She had deserved better.

***

"Lucy!" Dan cried. His voice echoed around the trees.

Lucy ran, bare-footed through the dark forest, searching for the source. She opened her mouth to call his name but no sound came out. The tangled canopy rippled above, drip-feeding dim moonlight across the leaves. The branches creaked in the wind.

"Lucy, please!" he called, a tone of panic in his voice.

Lucy turned and ran towards his voice. Her foot struck something hard and she fell to the floor, landing hard on her ribs. She swept the leaves aside, revealing the train tracks beneath.

"*Lucy!*" he cried.

***

The lock turned, snapping Lucy out of her dream. Marissa stood in the threshold.

"Get changed, the Queen wants you," she said, staring at Lucy impatiently.

Lucy clambered to her feet.

"What for?" she said, faintly registering that night had fallen outside.

"Just hurry up, or you'll be going like that," said Marissa.

Lucy turned her back to the woman and quickly changed into her uniform and boots.

"What's with your arm?" said Marissa, eyeing up the red lesions.

"You never seen eczema before?" said Lucy, hastily pulling her top half on.

Marissa grunted. They exited the glass cubicle and Marissa led Lucy back upstairs to the top floor, taking her through security again before they entered the Queen's apartment where Lopez was already waiting.

"Ah, here she is, the woman of the hour. You've had quite the time, haven't you?" said the Queen, waving her notebook at her.

Lucy stared at the notebook despondently.

"Did you get some rest?" said the Queen, setting it down on her desk.

"A little," said Lucy.

"You'll need your energy tonight, Lucy. I'm giving you the opportunity to prove yourself. Maurice has claimed you're special; immune, even, and I need to know how much truth is in that. So tonight you will be Marissa's body guard. She has something important to retrieve from the city, and you're going to make sure she gets back alive. If you're successful, Marissa will launch a flare by dawn," said the Queen.

"Will we get weapons?" said Lucy, glancing at Lopez.

"Lucy, you *are* the weapon," said the Queen.

"I'm not – it doesn't work like that, it depends on the creature," urged Lucy.

"Marissa will be armed, in case you try anything," said the Queen.

"What about the Major?" said Lucy.

"Major Lopez will not be joining you. He's my insurance, honey, in case you feel tempted to flee. Last I heard, he sacrificed his own escape to stop those brutish soldiers from killing you in some forest? What a sweet guy," said the Queen.

"I did my duty as a soldier," said Lopez.

"Alright, then you're a sweet soldier. Either way, dear Lucy here owes you. Don't worry Ms Young, so long as you're back by sunrise, we'll all be fine," said the Queen.

"And if I fail the mission?" asked Lucy.

"If you come back empty handed, there will be non-lethal consequences for you and the Major. You will each have a chance to earn your citizenship, but there will be a punishment element. The real issue is if you don't come back at all. In that case I'd have to execute the poor Major and I'll be honest with you, honey, it would be very slow, and very public."

"You gotta send a message with these things," agreed Marissa, finishing her rifle checks.

"I bid you both good luck. Best hurry, only a few hours until sunrise," said the Queen.

Marissa led Lucy from the room, and they descended the stairs to the darkened atrium where the bony gatekeeper met them. He escorted them outside and cranked the razor wire wedge open. The night was cold but dry, around forty degrees Fahrenheit, Lucy reckoned. The moon was a thick, bright crescent, around two-thirds full. Lucy paused in the forecourt at marveled at the density of stars that hung over the blacked-out skyscrapers.

"Hey, get a move on," called Marissa, who had finished crawling through the wedge. Lucy followed, dusting off the snow from her hands and knees as she emerged the other side and hastened after the woman.

Lucy and Marissa slipped through the bus blockade onto the deserted street, where Marissa unlocked a parked van. The engine echoed off empty buildings as Marissa took them across the deserted, snowy streets of Brooklyn. They drove for around ten minutes, during which time, Lucy spotted only one candle.

"This is us," said Marissa, parking up by an intersection and climbing out.

NYU Lutheran Medical Centre read the sign above the hospital entrance, across the way. The street looked as if it had been frozen in time, during the bacterial outbreak. Abandoned cars and ambulances clogged the final approach to the hospital. Algae dotted the external walls and windows, and a thin vine hung across the entrance sign.

"Why are we at the Emergency Department? Are we getting medicine?" whispered Lucy.

"Pff, please, we took that months ago. We're here for the blood bank," said Marissa, opening the van's rear door and retrieving a crowbar.

"But it'll be unusable – the refrigerators will have failed months ago," said Lucy, scanning the street.

"The science team said they can make it work. They tend to get what they want," said Marissa, slamming the van door and heading for the entrance.

She forced the crowbar between the hospital's sliding doors and levered them apart. She then placed the bar horizontally between them, propping the doors open.

"The last team we sent in here didn't make it back, so you'd better be immune or we're both fucked," said Marissa, handing Lucy a flashlight. She turned the rifle's light on, then ducked under the bar and headed inside the gloomy reception.

The floor was covered in patches of frosted plant growth – a mixture of pale blue moss, shrubs, wild grasses, and saplings. Amidst the new growth, abandoned bed trollies lay overturned, with algae and moss growing on them. A red phone on the side of the wall hung off the hook. Lucy stepped on a badge, which crackled underfoot. She flinched, seeing the nurse's ID, and kicked it aside.

"This way," said Marissa, illuminating a sign to the blood bank. Lucy followed her further into the building. As they progressed through the corridors, pockets of wild grass and winter heather appeared. Purple ivy stretched across the walls and ceiling, similar to that which Lucy had seen by the farm. The leaves were serrated, and had the texture of a pig's ear – like a piece of tough leather, covered in very fine pale hairs. Lucy prodded one of the leaves with the tip of her flashlight. A shiver passed down the length of the ivy. Marissa raised her rifle and backed away. The shiver returned, rippling through the ivy back towards the afflicted leaf. The leaf shuddered and detached. It fell to the ground and shriveled, turning pale lilac. In its place on the ivy, something was wriggling out of the bud. Lucy backed away as a wet, black hornet slithered out of the broken stem and settled on the branch, pruning its glistening body.

The hornet shook itself out and unfurled its wings. With a flutter it took off, hovering unstably as it assessed Lucy and Marissa. Marissa moved to raise her rifle but Lucy stayed her hand.

"Don't provoke it," whispered Lucy.

The hornet loomed closer and settled on Marissa's ghost-white neck. The woman's eyes bulged as Lucy restrained her from swatting it. Lucy moved her hand slowly towards the creature, finger and thumb ready to pinch its wings, but as she approached a flap on the tip of the hornet's tail peeled back, revealing a thick stinger. As the hornet raised its tail, preparing to strike Marissa's neck, they were bathed in pale blue light. The strip light above them had flickered on. It was covered in moss, which glowed pastel blue as the light shone through it, the brightness ebbing and flowing in a distinctive oscillation. The hornet retracted its stringer and took off, zig-zagging upwards until it landed on the moss. The hornet pruned its wings once again and the light faded out completely. The hornet buzzed loudly and Marissa shone her rifle light on the ceiling, but the insect couldn't move; its feet had become stuck in the blue moss.

"Next time, don't touch the ivy. This way," said Marissa, pressing on down the overgrown corridor towards the stairwell.

As they crossed the doorway, the temperature changed. The air became humid, and there was a putrid-sweet scent of fermenting manure. Droplets of water from the stairs above fell onto Lucy's head and shoulders. By the sounds of it, water was dripping from the stairs below, too, into a pool of sorts. The windows were steamed up.

Marissa loosened her jumpsuit as they descended the steps towards the blood bank. The dripping noises grew louder. Spiraling ivy lined their route, the leaves of which darkened with each floor they descended, gradually turning from purple to midnight blue.

As they reached the basement they halted on the staircase; the entire level was submerged. Water lapped at the upper steps, barely a foot from the ceiling.

"Burst water main?" said Lucy, casting her light down the steps at the submerged doorway.

She marveled at the steam rising from the water's surface. Water droplets fell from the ivy onto the black water below, where the plant's roots disappeared. Jade-colored reeds protruded above the surface and arched over themselves as they brushed against the ceiling. Among the reeds grew lily pads. They were violet-colored, shaped like a half-bowl, and stuck to the walls. A bristly green stamen arched over each bowl akin to a hovering chopstick.

"How come it's warm?" said Marissa, casting her light across the dripping plant life.

"My money's on thermogenic plants. In Wisconsin there were these skunk cabbages which used to melt the snow so they could pollinate. Maybe these plants have appropriated some of those genes," said Lucy.

"Luckily for you they've turned it into a sauna," said Marissa.

"What?" said Lucy.

"You're going in there," Marissa retorted.

"You can't be serious," said Lucy.

"The blood bank's down there and I'm sure as hell not going in - you're the immune one."

Lucy stared at the misting, black water.

"This is insane," she said, shuddering.

"Going back to the Queen empty handed would be insane. This is better, trust me," said Marissa.

Lucy picked up a defunct pager from the stairs and tossed it into the water. She and Marissa trained their lights on the ripples. The waves radiated outwards and lapped against the walls until they'd dissipated entirely.

"Where's the blood bank?" said Lucy.

"How would I know? Read the signs," said Marissa.

"In the dark?" said Lucy.

"Your flashlight's water resistant," said Marissa.

"My clothes aren't," said Lucy.

"I guess that's a fair point. Let's check the staff changing rooms. Someone in the place will have a swimming costume, I guarantee it – it's a hospital. They're all health nerds," said Marissa.

"Surely we could just look for blood someplace else – another hospital, perhaps?" said Lucy, as Marissa led them up a level and into the frosty corridor.

"No time," said Marissa.

"But –" began Lucy.

Marissa cut her off.

"This is non-negotiable, so get over it. Either we get you some gear, or you go in like that and freeze when you come out. I really don't care," said Marissa.

They weaved between empty trolleys and beds, taking care not to disturb the ivy as they searched for the staff area.

"Here," said Marissa, crossing behind a reception desk and through the private doorway, revealing men's and women's changing rooms. They entered the female section and set about searching the lockers, most of which were locked.

"You got anything?" said Marissa, rifling through the few bags on the benches.

"Not really," said Lucy, inspecting a gym bag full of running kit.

Marissa appeared over her shoulder.

"That'll do," she said, grabbing the bag and leaving the room.

"What about my eyes – and my hair?" protested Lucy, hurrying to keep up as Marissa swung into the men's locker room.

"Way ahead of you," said Marissa, poking around the discarded items. "Aha! Seek and you shall find," she cheered, tossing Lucy a bag containing goggles, trunks, and a second towel. "Oh, and grab some empty bags – we'll need to transport the blood in something," added Marissa, as she shook out a couple of backpacks and slung them over her shoulder.

"How much blood are we taking?" said Lucy.

"As much as they've got. Now come on, clock's ticking," said Marissa, grabbing a third bag and heading for the exit.

They returned to the basement level where Lucy stripped off. Goose pimples faded from her skin as her body relaxed in the humid air.

"You always had it?" said Marissa, staring at Lucy's back as she changed.

"Had what?" said Lucy, pulling on the male swim trunks.

"Eczema," said Marissa, tilting her head.

Lucy craned her neck and examined the base of her spine, where a band of red lesions spanned both hips.

"Oh, yeah, it flares up sometimes," she muttered, hastily pulling the running top over her head.

"I think blood's down the corridor on the right," said Marissa, squatting and examining the sign above the basement doorway.

Lucy pulled the rubbery swimming cap over her hair. She wrestled it down until it pinged into place across her forehead.

"Tie this around your waist," said Marissa, pulling a fire hose from the wall.

"For real?" said Lucy.

"Give three sharp tugs on it if you get into trouble and I'll haul you in," said Marissa.

Lucy tied the red hose around her waist as best she could. The nozzle poked up off the end, awkwardly pressing into her abdomen.

Lucy picked up her flashlight and slung three empty backpacks over her shoulder. She descended down onto the first submerged step, allowing the water to engulf her feet and ankles. It was warm – inviting almost, save for the darkness, and the plant life. Lucy pulled the goggles over her eyes and waded down up to her waist then cast off from the steps and swam towards the door.

"I can't find the handle," Lucy called to Marissa, who was covering her with the rifle.

"You gotta swim for it. Suck it up, we don't have all night," said Marissa.

Lucy took a deep breath and ducked below the surface. She squeezed the air pockets out of the empty bags, which dragged in the water. The green reeds stretched to the floor, which was around two meters below the surface. Lucy transferred the torch into her bag-holding arm and pulled the door open, then swam through into the submerged corridor.

The trunk of the ivy stretched along the length of the wall in both directions, where it regularly branched off into a vertical root structure – much like a mangrove tree. Its leaves were gone, but the thick, midnight blue trunks were studded with tiny white flowers. The base of each trunk ended in a large tubular 'bucket'. Each trunk-bucket had a waxy-looking lid. The majority were lifted like toilet seats. They appeared hollow and glowed violet as Lucy illuminated each one in turn, until she reached the first with a closed lid. The flashlight revealed a small, curled mass contained within the bucket, which briefly belched out a gas bubble, causing the lid to flap open a few inches.

Lucy swam over to the bucket and treaded water. It belched again and the lid lifted up. She glimpsed inside: a dead rat, wrapped in fine violet tentacles. Lucy swam to the surface and took a gasp of air. The blood bank was along and right, as Marissa had said. She swam forwards but after several more meters felt a jolt across her waist; she'd reached the extent of the fire hose. Spotting a trolley below, she swam down and re-tied the hose around its metal handlebar, before continuing onwards, untethered.

She turned the door handle to the blood bank and swam into the room. Tall refrigerators lined the walls. Charts and packing boxes were scattered across the worktops and floor. Lucy pulled open the nearest fridge. With the flashlight tucked under her arm, she stuffed bags of crimson blood into a backpack. It became heavy, quickly. She zipped it up, and let it sink onto a worktop in the center of the room, then surfaced to catch her breath. Bubbles breached the surface from the far side of the room as another plant trunk discharged its gases.

Lucy dived down and filled the second and third backpacks from the next fridges, then left the room. As she swam back towards the main corridor, a clicking sound pricked her ears. She turned, mid-water. Her flashlight reached down the length of the corridor, illuminating the reeds and ivy trunks within. The clicking sounded again. She swiveled around and shone her light in the other direction. The double-door at the far end was swinging shut. She kicked away and more clicks ensued as a limbless creature slithered out from the far thicket of reeds.

Its body was long, and moved like an eel's. It seemed impervious to her flashlight as it slowly snaked towards her. The anemic creature was easily as long as her. A ridge of fins lined the second half of its tail, which tapered to a point.

As Lucy swam harder the creature clicked louder and sped up. She stopped immediately and waited, suspended in the water, as the creature approached. A trunk halfway along the corridor let out an almighty belch and the creature swiveled around, darting towards the source. Lucy seized the opportunity and made a dash for the trolley. She slung the backpacks onto the trolley and tugged the hose sharply three times. The hose tautened and the trolley began to wheel towards the double doors. The clicking sound resumed in the distance, getting louder as it approached the intersection. Lucy spun around, training the torch on the junction as the clicking grew louder, trying to kick backwards as she watched.

With a clang, the trolley collided with the door frame behind her. The clicking erupted into a near drumroll as the creature sped towards the commotion. Lucy frantically paddled towards the door and pushed it open, straightening the trolley up for Marissa to reel in. She glanced down the corridor – the creature was swimming towards her with speed. Lucy grabbed her flashlight and hurled it towards the far end of the corridor like a Frisbee. It struck the hanging metal sign with a clatter, and dropped into the water below with a splash. The clicking creature spun around and ferreted towards the clatter as Lucy slipped through the doorway to the stairwell.

Lucy splashed out of the water and onto the steps, startling Marissa, who had hoisted the trolley up the first few steps and was retrieving the backpacks.

"Get away from the water!" cried Lucy, scrambling up onto the flat mid-story platform on the staircase.

Marissa grabbed the bags and leapt backwards from the water, letting the trolley slip back down with a bump. Marissa grabbed her rifle and trained it on the black, misting water, and the basement doorway.

"Get changed, quickly," she ordered.

Lucy dried herself hastily, stripping off and scrubbing the water away, wincing as the towel rubbed the bruises and lesions on her malnourished body. A loud clicking echoed through the water and the basement door flapped open. Marissa backed away further from the water's edge.

An anemic, veiny webbed paw slapped out onto the first step above the water line. Marissa fired at it, tearing the paw in two. The creature's limb retracted as a cloudy, milky liquid floated to the surface. She stared at the black water, waiting for the ripples to settle. A second paw slapped onto the step and Marissa fired again. Lucy grabbed her clothes and raced up to the next level, where she hastily pulled her uniform back on. Marissa followed, clutching the blood bags, and covering the stairs below. They stumbled along the corridor to the nearest desk island, where Marissa paused.

"Sling these two on. I'll take the third," said Marissa, lowering her rifle and handing Lucy two of the backpacks.

"Freeze!" cried a voice from the darkness.

Lucy squinted as a flashlight dazzled them.

"Shit," muttered Marissa, raising one arm in surrender.

"Don't," came another voice from the side, catching Marissa's stealthy reach for her trigger.

"Toss it," demanded the man ahead.

Marissa reluctantly slid her rifle across the floor, shunting it a token few feet towards the men. She raised both hands and Lucy copied.

Behind the flashlights, Lucy could just about make out two men up ahead, and one to their side. The men appeared to have hand guns, and looked like civilians.

"What's in the bags?" called the man ahead of them.

"Blood," said Marissa.

"For real?" said the man.

"Yup," said Marissa. She slowly unzipped her backpack and tilted it towards them. The men shone the spotlights on the blood bags.

"What you doing with three backpacks full of blood?" said the man.

"Fuck you, that's what," said Marissa.

"I reckon we want them bags. Toss 'em over," said the man.

"Not gonna happen," said Marissa.

"Toss 'em or we shoot," said the man.

"You shoot us and there's blood everywhere. Then the creatures come."

"We'll be gone by then, it's you they'll find," said the man.

"So then what's the point? If all that happens here is you kill us, then that seems a waste of your resources. You got infinite ammo?"

"We got plenty of ammo," said the man.

"Uh-huh, sounds that way," said Marissa.

"Lie down on the ground," said the man.

"Fuck you," said Marissa.

The man to their side edged closer, his light growing brighter.

"You want me to take them, boss?"

"Yeah, but the bitch is right – save your ammo. We'll take them old school," said the man, closing in.

Lucy swiped her hand across the ivy, showering the floor in withering violet leaves. She grabbed Marissa's arm and the pair turned and ran. Moss-covered strip lights flickered on overhead, filling the corridor with blue illumination as the men chased after them.

"What the hell?" cried one of the men, as the sound of buzzing hornets filled the air.

The men's shouts of confusion turned to shouts of pain as the hornets attacked. They fired hopelessly at the nimble insects, further antagonizing the swarm.

Lucy and Marissa sped down the corridor, aided by moonlight reaching through the windows, until they reached a fire exit. Lucy kicked it open and they clambered down the metal staircase, jumping onto the snow below.

"This way!" urged Marissa, sprinting towards their van across the street.

She whacked on the ignition and hauled the vehicle around as gun shots rang out from the emergency exit. They sped away, out of view of the hospital, and out of the gunner's range.

"Wait, where are you taking us?" said Lucy, as they diverged from their original route.

"We've got one more stop to make," said Marissa, climbing through the gears.

***

Marissa brought the van to a halt outside an imposing stone building. *Appellate Division · Supreme Court of the State of New York · Second Department.* The inscription was writ large across the top of the building, spanning its entire width. Slender, moon-made shadows clung to the pillars framing the entrance, accentuating its height.

Marissa grabbed a spare flashlight and jumped out, drawing her handgun as she marched up the stone. Lucy stuck close by her as she pushed through two consecutive sets of metal-and-glass doors. The golden door frames matched the gilded lettering across the glass, which reiterated the building's purpose.

Marissa struck her handgun against the frame of the metal-detector with a clang as she swaggered through. The building was pitch-black inside, save for the light from Marissa's flashlight, which jerked unevenly as she marched.

As they rounded the corridor the light fell across fresh moss, which was growing along the skirting boards. Feeding off it were three tortoises with beige-green shells. The sight of the reptiles startled Marissa, who fired her pistol, killing the first outright.

"Shit," she cursed, freezing and assessing the other creatures' reactions.

While the remaining tortoises seemed indifferent to the loss of their comrade, several lice scurried out from beneath the skirting board and began feasting on the fresh carcass. Marissa scanned her light across the rest of the hallway, checking for other signs of life, but there were none, save for the moss and algae covering the walls in shades of blue and purple.

"Come on," said Marissa, pressing on.

They reached another golden door, with a fresh inscription above it: *Courtroom One*. Marissa kicked the door open and stormed in, flashlight and pistol raised.

The courtroom was cavernous, with a ceiling two stories high, ornately decorated with patterned square tiles. The walls were made of grey-white stone, the bottom half of which was clad in oak paneling. Rows of seats filled the room, divided by a central aisle. At the far end was the judge's bench, which spanned the width of the room. The five judicial seats were framed by two flags – the Stars and Stripes on the left, and another which Lucy didn't recognize on the right.

A groan from the front of the room startled Lucy. Marissa trained her light on the upper left hand side, and made a beeline towards the sound.

Two figures sat slumped by the front. They were positioned behind the defendant's desk; handcuffed to their seats and to the table legs. Lucy gasped as she saw their uniforms – they were police officers. A rancid smell hit Lucy's nostrils as she approached; the female officer was dead. Her face was pale and emaciated. The carpet by her feet was blood soaked, where blood had pooled in her legs and burst through the skin. The male cop next to her whimpered as they approached, begging for mercy in a desert-dry voice.

"Officer Priestly, good to see you again," said Marissa, illuminating the terrified man's face.

"Please… just kill me," he stammered.

"Like you killed that kid? Come on, that'd be too easy. This is about *justice*, surely you've figured that out by now?" said Marissa.

"Help me," begged Priestly, looking past Marissa to Lucy.

"Don't listen to him. This man doesn't deserve help," said Marissa.

"Why are they here?" said Lucy, pulling her uniform over her nose.

"They're awaiting trial. Though it looks like she won't be testifying anymore," said Marissa, flicking the light at the dead cop.

"They're police officers," said Lucy, shocked.

"I know, it's disgusting. Someone though it'd be a good idea to give this scumbag a badge and a gun. He went and killed an unarmed teenage boy last year. There was phone footage of the kid surrendering and everything. Hands raised, on his knees. And yet Officer Priestly here still saw fit to shot him in the back three times. Why was that, Officer?"

Priestly whimpered.

"Yeah. You know why," said Marissa, holstering her pistol.

She knelt down and undid both sets of handcuffs. Priestly slumped to the ground, groaning, while Marissa stood back up.

"Case was due to go to court last year, but then the apocalypse happened. NYPD sensed that the satellites weren't coming back, and that the virus was out of control, so they abandoned the city. They retreated into their own enclave, barricading themselves off from everyone – including the National Guard. They horded food, weapons, and water, and waited for the virus and the creatures to kill the rest of us off. But it didn't get all of us, did it? And now we're the ones running the city, and the cops are scared, cos they're running out of food, and they know that when spring comes, there'll be a race for the city's remaining resources. So Priestly and his colleague here devised a genius plan to infiltrate our community and map the building, so they could take us down before winter ends. He cut his hair, even died it this lovely shade of brown, but our Queen recognized him immediately. She found them a couple of uniforms, and brought them here to await trial. But there's good news, Priestly, the Queen's decided to give you a reprieve – if you help us," said Marissa, tapping the man with her foot.

Priestly groaned.

"Kill me," he croaked.

"Oh, the Queen also asked me to inform you that we have your husband, Michael," said Marissa.

The cop's eyes widened.

"Impossible," he croaked.

Marissa pulled a phone from her pocket and played a short video clip, in which an unarmed man delivered a message directly to the camera, addressing Priestly by name, and begging him to comply.

Priestly wailed with despair.

"He came looking for you. Sweet, I know. Relax, Priestly, we're not gonna hurt him. He's an unarmed civilian, we'd never do that. He wants you back alive. So either you help us, or you're the one hurting him," said Marissa. She played the video again for good measure. "Do we have a deal?" she added.

Priestly nodded, wincing as he rubbed his stiff legs.

"Here's what's gonna happen, child-killer. You're gonna take us to your little police paradise hide out. We're gonna raid your medicine store which, we're reliably informed is on the top floor.

You're gonna get us in there. If we get this done by dawn, your fella – and hers – get to live, so we'd best get moving. Lucy, give the good Officer a hand, would you?" said Marissa.

Lucy helped the Officer to his feet. He yelped as his stiff joints stretched out. His breath was awful and his trousers stank of urine. He clung to Lucy like a crutch as she followed Marissa out of the courtroom.

***

Marissa gave Priestly a rehydration sachet in the van, followed by a cup of sugary, hot coffee from a thermos flask.

"Technically this wasn't for you, but I snuck us some extra," said Marissa, handing Lucy a mug of coffee with a wink. She poured herself a cup too, placed it in the cup holder, then hit the ignition.

Lucy held Priestly's coffee until it had cooled enough for him to resume drinking without scolding himself – his hands were weak, and his movements clumsy.

"Kill the car lights," said Priestly, after several minutes.

"We're still a couple of miles from the hotel," said Marissa.

"And they'll see us coming. Kill the lights. Go by the moonlight," insisted Priestly.

"They're staying in a hotel?" said Lucy.

"I know. Cops, right?" said Marissa, killing the lights as she took them deeper into Brooklyn.

"OK, nearly here. Take the next right," said Priestly, a while later.

"But it's straight on?" said Marissa.

"They'll hear us, they've got people watching the front. Take the back street, then we can cut through on foot," he insisted.

Marissa took them around to the parallel street and parked up outside an auto repair. It had a flat roof, behind which was a tall wire fence, and a little further back from that, a five-story hotel – the tallest building in the neighborhood.

"I'm not seeing any cut through," said Marissa.

"It's over the mechanic's roof. Then we climb the fence – it'll take us into the hotel parking lot. From there we can access the fire escape. That's the best way to the roof. From there we can go inside to the top floor and get to the medicines. Any other route and we're guaranteed to get caught," said Priestly.

"Take one of these," said Marissa, giving Lucy and Priestly a soaking-wet backpack each.

"What's in it?" said Priestly.

"Our get-out-of-jail card, to stop them shooting us," said Marissa, swinging on two additional backpacks herself.

"You should back the van up against the store – it'll give us a way to the roof," said Lucy, eyeing up the flat store front.

Marissa obliged, and the three clambered over the trunk, across the van's roof and onto the flat roof of the garage.

"Watch the skylight!" hissed Lucy, as Priestly swayed across the roof, his balance still weak.

They stumbled across the roof towards the metal fence. Lucy felt the scratchy felt gripping her boots as she disturbed the layer of snow above it.

"Who wants to try this first?" said Marissa.

"Check the end, there should be a supporting beam we can use as a foothold," said Lucy, edging along to the tip of the fence.

She swung around the side-pole and gripped the wire mesh with her hands, squeezing a boot tip into the mesh below. Her second foot slipped, causing her to rattle against the wire.

"Keep it down!" hissed Priestly.

Lucy moved each limb down individually, taking great care until she reached the diagonal support beam propping up the metal pole. From there, she tip-toed down the beam then jumped the last meter.

"Get ready to catch him," said Marissa, who was helping Priestly around the side of the fence above.

He placed a shaky hand onto the mesh, followed by a shaky foot. Gingerly, he lowered himself towards the diagonal beam, only to slip as he tried to transfer his weight. The cop fell two meters and landed hard on his back, his fall barely cushioned by the thin layer of snow.

Lucy fell upon him and stifled his yell with her hands. His pained eyes opened in confusion as he looked up at her imploringly. Marissa quickly caught up, landing quietly beside them. She opened a pocket on her vest and pulled out a syringe.

"What's that?" whispered Lucy.

"Something to help the pain," said Marissa, pulling back the cop's sleeve and threading the needle into his vein.

The cop gasped and sat up, panting.

"Gaaah, what's happening?" he spluttered.

"Sssh, keep it down. It's a family recipe - morphine and adrenaline. I thought you'd be needing it back at the courthouse but you limped on for quite a while, like the psychopath you are. It'll keep you going so you can help us do this, and we can get you back to your husband. That's the deal, child-killer," said Marissa, pulling him to his feet.

The cop gathered his thoughts then led them across the parking lot to the back of the darkened hotel. As quietly as possible, they stacked some empty beer crates beneath the fire escape so they could reach the ladder. They climbed the metal rungs to the first level of the escape, then tip-toed up the remaining flights of steps until they reached the fifth and final floor.

The view from the roof reminded Lucy of San Francisco during the curfews. Row upon row of darkened houses, with moonlight bouncing off black windows and idle cars – albeit these ones were snow-covered. The eastward night sky was starting to lighten, as the first tones of day crept onto the horizon. Sunrise was fast approaching.

"The medicine's this way," said Priestly, heading towards the roof door.

"Change of plans," said Marissa, barring his way.

"What do you mean?" said Priestly.

"We're staging an intervention. Your husband told us of your planned 'spring offensive' against the Queen, and we can't allow it to happen," said Marissa.

"What are you saying?" said Priestly.

"Open your backpack," said Marissa.

Priestly fumbled the zip open and lifted out a blood bag.

"What the hell?" he said, horrified.

"You know what that means, Priestly," said Marissa.

"This is madness. You call *me* a psychopath but you work for a monster!"

"A monster? She's our savior! She's brought order, shelter, and food to hundreds of starving people when your lot turned their backs on us all. She's a hero," said Marissa.

"In this hotel there are dozens of people who escaped your 'Queen'. The stories they've told are of abuse, violence, and humiliation. What your 'Queen' is running is a prison, filled with vulnerable people held hostage by fate," said Priestly.

"I won't deny we've got hostages. We've got two, in fact: your husband, and Lucy's sugar daddy. But the other occupants are *citizens*, who can come and go as they please. We protect innocent people, Priestly. I know that's something you struggle to relate to," said Marissa, thrusting a blood pack into Priestly's hands.

"Listen to me. This hotel is *full* of innocent people. If we do what I think you're asking, we're putting all of their lives in danger," implored Priestly.

"How many people?" said Lucy.

"Around three hundred," said Priestly.

"Three hundred cops," spat Marissa.

"Only a quarter of them are cops, the rest are their families and other civilians," said Priestly.

"Friends of cops, families of cops, same difference," said Marissa.

"I won't do it," said Priestly, shaking his head.

"Sure you will, if you want to save your husband," said Marissa.

Priestly's eyes began to water with despair.

"Same goes for you, immune-girl. Get pouring or the Major dies at dawn," said Marissa.

Lucy stared from Marissa, to the backpack, to the cop. Marissa drew her pistol, then drew a knife, which she handed to Lucy. She pointed to the AC vents.

"Cut the bags, and toss them down the chutes. That's all you gotta do. Then we fire the flare, go back to the Queen, and save your hostages."

"And if we refuse?" said Priestly.

"If you refuse, I'll do it myself. Then I'll drive back to the Queen without you. I'll tell her you disobeyed her orders, and it'll be a slow and painful death for your husband and the Major," said Marissa.

"You're making us chose one life over hundreds," whimpered Priestly.

"You're absolutely right, child-killer. It's a choice," said Marissa.

"If I do this, my husband lives?" said Priestly, staring at the blood pack.

"That's what I said," retorted Marissa.

"I'll do it. Pass me the packs," said Lucy.

Lucy took the first bag from Priestly's hand and held it over the vent. She stabbed it then tossed it down the chute, where it clattered against the sides and landed somewhere inside the ceiling duct below with a damp thud.

"Alright. We're officially on the clock," said Marissa.

Lucy stabbed and chucked the bags as quickly as she could, with Priestly feeding them through from each backpack. They spread the payload across vents as Marissa instructed. Within two minutes each backpack had been emptied, and Lucy stood clutching the knife in her bloodied hand.

"Good. Now cut him," said Marissa.

"What?" said Lucy.

"Cut the cop," said Marissa.

"What the hell's wrong with you?" said Lucy.

"Do it, or I'll throw your flare off the side of this building. If the sun starts to rise and there's not been any kind of signal, I don't think the Queen will treat your hostages too kindly," said Marissa.

"Hold still. I'm sorry about this," said Lucy, turning to Priestly.

She slashed his cheek with the tip of the blade. She tried to scratch him lightly, but the blade was sharp. Blood seeped from the cut.

"Alright, we're done here. Well done, Priestly. I'll tell the Queen you did your job. Your husband's life will be spared. See you back at HQ," said Marissa, heading for the staircase.

"You're leaving us?" cried Lucy.

"Those creatures are coming and you're both covered in blood, I'm outta here. Wait, did I not mention? This is the second part of your test, Lucy. Get the cop back to the Queen by dawn, or the Major dies. Cya round. The flare's in the bag. It buys you an extra thirty minutes," said Marissa, dumping the dry backpack and disappearing down the staircase.

"How far are we from the Queen's HQ?" said Lucy, turning to Priestly urgently.

"To hell with that, I need to warn my people," replied the bleeding cop. "Hey!-"

Lucy clamped her hand over his mouth and pinned the knife to his throat.

"Shut the *hell* up. If we get caught, there's no way we'll make it back to the Queen," said Lucy, uncovering the cop's mouth but keeping the blade in position.

"Screw the Queen, we need to warn the people in this building,"

"Yes, but not if it's going to get us caught – if that happens, Lopez dies. Your guy may be safe, but mine isn't," said Lucy.

"He's one life – you can't put him above hundreds of innocent people," rasped Priestly.

"You damned hypocrite!" spat Lucy.

"That's different. That was my *husband*. Who are you saving? Your life partner? A dear friend? Your brother?"

"No, he's–"

"He's nothing, then," spat Priestly.

"He's about the only person left who believes in what this country used to stand for," said Lucy.

"I don't buy it," said Priestly.

"Fuck you," said Lucy, edging the blade closer.

"I'm a cop, I know when people are lying," hissed Priestly.

"You really think the Queen's gonna spare your husband if you don't make it back?" said Lucy.

"You're changing the subject," said Priestly.

"What will I tell him, if you're not there? It sounds like he can't bear to live without you," said Lucy.

Concern washed over Priestly's face.

"You wouldn't," said Priestly, weakly.

"I already let my life partner die, and I can't be that person again," insisted Lucy.

"The truth at last," said Priestly.

"You're still bleeding," said Lucy, pointing to his cheek, with the blade. "If you want to survive the night, I'm your best bet. I'm immune to the creatures. I can get you to your husband alive," said Lucy.

"Let me warn my people first, we're running out of time," implored Priestly.

"I can't risk losing you," said Lucy.

"Then use the flare. Fire it into the vent – the smoke will lead them to the blood. Do it and I'll come with you," said Priestly.

"We're miles from the Queen's place and it's getting lighter already, I can't throw away thirty minutes!" said Lucy.

"I can get us a car," said Priestly.

"Double-cross me and you die," said Lucy.

"Like you said, I'm bleeding, and my husband's still vulnerable. You're my best bet," said Priestly.

Lucy stared into the man's eyes for a moment, then released her grip. He slumped down the vent and regained his breath. She grabbed the flare and fired it into the nearest AC unit. It smashed against the piping and out of sight.

"That should raise the alarm. Now come on – we need to get to the ground before this place is overrun," said Lucy, hastening towards the stairs.

They fled down the exit, rattling down each floor as quickly as they could. As they wound past the third story, a bell sounded loudly inside. The pitch and rhythm varied slightly, suggesting it was hand-held. Muffled shouts and cries spread across the building as more residents awoke to the alarm and roused their peers.

"Hurry!" urged Lucy as Priestly lagged behind.

She finished the final set of stairs, descended the end ladder onto the crates below, and jumped to the ground, regaining her balance in time to catch Priestly as he followed.

"That way!" cried Priestly, pointing down the side of the hotel.

As the pair skirted the length of the building, Lucy heard an engine running. She stopped at the periphery and stuck her head around the corner. A man was sat behind the wheel of an SUV, shouting through the open window to people on the street. A child was running from the hotel towards the passenger door. A woman stood on the sidewalk, shouting at someone else inside to hurry.

"The safe house is too close, we need to get further away from the blood!" cried the man.

"I'll distract them – you get to the kid in the back. She's our leverage. Go!" cried Priestly.

Lucy scampered to the far side of the street, into the shadows, and skulked towards the parked vehicles as Priestly staggered down the sidewalk towards the woman.

"Josie, take me with you!" cried Priestly, waving his arms dramatically.

Lucy drew level with the rear passenger door.

"Oh my god, Leo!" cried Josie, as Priestly ran towards her.

"He's bleeding!" cried the father, from the car.

Lucy darted to the car and pulled the rear passenger door open. She hauled the young girl out pressed the bloodied knife to her neck.

"Jesus!" cried the man.

Lucy stood in front of the car.

"Do what we say and she'll be fine. Now get in the back!" shouted Lucy.

The father jumped out of the front seat, his hands raised imploringly.

"Please, please let her go," he begged.

"Get in the back! Priestly, you're driving," yelled Lucy.

Priestly hurried to the driver's seat.

"In the back – both of you!" Lucy yelled to the mother, who was clutching her remaining child by the shoulders, terrified. More people were beginning to run through the hotel lobby, heading for the street. The mother and daughter hurried into the back of the car. Lucy dragged the quivering hostage child into the front with her, drawing her onto her lap and sealing the door. Priestly slammed the accelerator and pulled them away, as confused shouts called after them.

Priestly pulled on his seatbelt as he drove. Lucy clocked this and ordered the child to draw hers over both of them.

"What the hell are you doing?" cried the mother from the back.

"Saving my husband," said Priestly, as he sped through the streets.

"Please let my daughter go," begged the husband, from the back.

"She's fine. We're taking you to safety," said Lucy.

"You're covered in blood! You're a magnet for the creatures!" cried the father.

"Then gimme a rag," said Lucy.

The father passed her a towel from the floor. Lucy wiped her hands and knife clean, then tossed the towel out of the window. The tip of the sun was edging onto the winter horizon.

"Gimme another," said Lucy.

"I don't have another," said the man.

"Then make one," said Lucy, discretely re-sheathing the knife.

He tore a strip off his shirt sleeve and passed it to Lucy. She dabbed the excess blood from Priestly's cheek then tossed it from the window, while a new layer formed along the cut.

"It was you, wasn't it? The blood in the vents – you did it!" cried Josie.

"I didn't have a choice," protested Priestly.

"You've condemned them all!" said Josie.

"We gave them a warning. It's more of a chance than they were ever going to get without us," said Lucy.

Lucy spotted two beams of light twirling across the night sky. The top of the Queen's building was lit up like a beacon.

"You can't be serious – we're not going back, you can't take us back!" protested the father.

"You've been here before?" said Lucy, aghast.

"Christ, it took us two months to escape. She's going to punish us!" the man whimpered.

The Queen's building came into view. *Refugees Welcome* was written across the top floor windows in giant iridescent paint. Rap music blared as they approached.

"Shit!" cried Priestly, as a beast leapt in front of the headlights. He swerved heavily, hitting the curb at speed, and flipping the SUV onto its side. It skidded through the snow into a parked vehicle. The collision projected the unbuckled father out of his seat and into the car's roof, before he crashed down in a heap by the passenger window, to the screams of his wife and daughter.

Lucy and the girl hung sideways in the front seat, suspended above Priestly, whose forehead was bleeding. Lucy's eyes widened in horror as the beast reappeared in the van's headlights, bounding towards them.

Gun shots rained down in the darkness and a series of bullets embedded themselves in the beast, felling it in the street. Lucy pushed the passenger door upwards, thrusting it open.

"You're gonna have to climb out. I'm gonna leave the seat belt in place, you gotta wriggle. See that gearbox there? Put your foot on that. Good – now see the door's open? You gotta climb to the edge, then jump down onto the sidewalk. Your mom and sister will be right behind you I promise, now go," said Lucy, helping lift the girl up to the door ledge.

Placing her own foot on the gearbox, Lucy unclipped her seatbelt. She leaned down and unclipped Priestly's, too, then dragged him to his feet. She slapped his face several times, and his eyes fluttered open.

"Hey, stay with me. Nearly there. I'm gonna climb up, you gotta follow," said Lucy.

She hauled herself up to the door ledge then braced her feet and one hand against the frame. With tremendous effort, she reached down and pulled Priestly upward.

He climbed, groggily, with much coercion, until Lucy could reach his belt and drag him over the lip of the doorway. He slumped over the edge and onto the snowy sidewalk. Lucy jumped down and helped him up.

"Help us, please!" cried the woman, who was still inside the vehicle.

Having gotten her second daughter out, she was trying in vain to shift her husband. More guns shots rang out from the surrounding buildings. Lucy climbed into the doorway and reached down, pulling the woman out.

"Get your kids to safety – I'll help your husband," shouted Lucy.

Then woman stumbled onto the sidewalk.

"There's a gap between the buses. Get inside the building – and take him with you," Lucy ordered, pointing the mother to the dazed Priestly.

Lucy dropped to the ground and forced the SUV trunk open. She clicked the uppermost backseat down and leaned over. The father was coming around, groaning.

"Give me your hand!" she called, glancing at the busses, as the group weaved between them.

The man reached up, feebly. Like Priestly, he was bleeding from the head. Lucy grasped his hand and hauled, but the man screamed out in pain; his shoulder was pinned beneath the broken driver's seat. Lucy tried to shift the seat but it just caused more pain.

Bullets rang out nearby.

"I'm gonna try lift the seat again – be ready to move your arm clear. One, two, three!" cried Lucy, heaving against the buckled seat rail.

The man cried out in pain, moving no distance at all. Lucy leaped to the ground and tackled the rear passenger seat, pulling it back vigorously until it snapped away, revealing the man's bloodied face. His arm was crushed beneath the seat in front, and Lucy could see no way to free it. The man reached out and Lucy clasped his hand in empathy. He looked at her imploringly.

"Help me – please. My daughters, help me!" cried the man, tears in his eyes.

A roar echoed across the street, followed by a second. Fear washed over Lucy as the two beasts bounded towards her. Her fleeting sense of immunity evaporated as the gnashing creatures tore towards her with intent.

"I'm sorry!" she cried.

Lucy released the man's hand, and ran for the blockade. As she fled between the busses, she saw bullets fell only one of the creatures; the second leapt into the open trunk.

She emerged from the busses and ran across the forecourt to the razor wire wedge, which the gaunt gatekeeper had cranked open in anticipation.

"Close it!" she cried, as she crawled through into the HQ side and sprinted for the building.

Gasping for breath, she hurtled into the atrium, where Marissa was waiting with the escapees.

"Where – where is he?" said the mother, looking at Lucy in disbelief.

"I'm so sorry, he was already gone," said Lucy, swallowing and staring at the floor.

The mother collapsed in a fit of grief. The two daughters looked lost beside her. A guard placed a hand on the woman's shoulder and helped her up, taking her to a sofa in the lobby.

"Where's Priestly? He needs green paste," said Lucy, breathlessly.

"They're dealing with him," said Marissa.

"And Lopez?" said Lucy.

Marissa bowed her head, solemnly.

"We never got the flare signal. He didn't make it – I'm sorry," she said.

Lucy's mouth turned dry and she sagged into a chair, waves of denial crashing over her as the new sank in.

"You did what you could. Get some rest, it's a fresh day tomorrow," said Marissa.

A guard directed Lucy towards the stairwell. She rose from her seat in a daze and followed his steer, climbing two flights of stairs until they peeled off onto the new level. The guard led her onto a floor with multiple segmented glass offices, similar to the one she'd stayed in previously. Lucy stared at her boots as the guard led her down the corridor. He unlocked a cubicle and nudged Lucy inside. It smelled of urine and gas, but it was warm.

"Lucy?" came a familiar voice.

She looked up as Lopez wrapped his arms around her. He checked her for injuries, then guided her to the floor.

"You came back," he said, clasping her by the shoulders with immense gratitude.

"You're alive," said Lucy distantly.

"Thanks to you," said Lopez.

Lucy took in their glass cubicle. Three strangers lay asleep on the floor around them.

"Are you OK? What did they make you do?" said Lopez, scratching his arm.

Lucy pulled his sleeve back and stared at the red lesions covering his skin.

"It's nothing," said Lopez, moving to re-cover his arm, but Lucy stopped him. She held up her own arm next to his, and pulled her sleeve back.

"You've got the same," he whispered, glancing around.

"This is like what happened to Jackson," said Lucy.

"But we didn't get infected – we only swallowed the powder," said Lopez.

"Maybe this is a side effect?" said Lucy.

"How long do we have? Jackson got weak quickly," said Lopez.

"Her condition was complicated. We might have another day, but it's definitely spreading," said Lucy.

"Can we get more white powder?" said Lopez.

"I tried that with Jackson and it didn't save her – I think it might be the cause," said Lucy.

Lopez stared at their spreading lesions, a grim look across his face.

"We need a cure – fast," said the Major.

FOUR

South

"Drink this, sweetie, you need to keep your strength up," said her mom.

Lucy sat up in her bed and reached out two small, shaky hands for the beaker. She had no appetite but forced down a few sips of cool soda. Her mom pressed a hand to her forehead and frowned sympathetically.

"You're burning up. I'm gonna call the school – no way you're going in today," said her mother, taking the beaker back.

"I'll call them – you stay here," said Lopez, giving Lucy's shoulder a squeeze and leaving the room. He was wearing jeans. He suited them.

A doctor entered and placed a thermometer under Lucy's tongue and a stethoscope against her back.

"This is the third day in a row," said Lucy's mother, putting her hands on her hips and tilting her head.

"Her heart beat's regular. Temperature looks OK, too. Is there anything you want to tell me, young lady?" said the doctor.

Lucy scrunched up her Disney blanket and pulled it closer to her chin, shaking her head.

"Would you mind giving us a minute?" the doctor added.

"Of course, doc," replied Lucy's mom, graciously. She stepped out into the hall, where she introduced herself to Dan. He was in ceremonial uniform, and clutching a bouquet of lilies. He peered through the doorway, looking concerned.

Lucy sat up to wave but the doctor drew a curtain around the bed. He lowered his voice confidentially.

"It's OK if you're not feeling sick, I won't be mad. Maybe there's something else making you not want to go to school?" asked the doctor, softly.

Lucy chewed her lip. The doctor tilted his ear towards her.

"I don't want mommy to go back," whispered Lucy.

***

The cubicle lock clicked and Lucy opened her eyes. Lopez entered, followed by three Chinese strangers clutching blankets and sleeping bags. They argued between themselves over who took which part of the floor, while Lopez knelt by Lucy.

"What happened to you?" said Lucy, looking at Lopez's black eye.

"It's fine. Here, I brought you some bread," replied Lopez, handing her two fistfuls of pitta.

"How'd you get so much?" said Lucy.

"For a prison, this place caters well," said Lopez.

"What time is it?" said Lucy.

"It's dusk."

"I was out for the whole day?"

"You got back at dawn, so no wonder," said Lopez.

"I didn't hear you leave," said Lucy.

"I'm surprised – it was a noisy exit. They wanted you to work, but I suggested you'd live longer if you got more than thirty minutes of sleep each day. They took it well," said Lopez, pointing to his eye.

"Thank you," said Lucy, blushing. She tore off a chunk of bread. It tasted salty. "What did they make you do?"

"This place is insane. They're growing plants on levels four and six, and they've re-plumbed the building to recycle all its water. It's like they've rounded up all the nerds in NYC and given them a purpose in life. Some of them seem pretty psyched about it, too. It's the weirdest thing. The nerds have got teams of grunts working for them. They have a lot of power, and they know it. Of course, the problem with glass cubicles is that when they abuse their newfound power everyone can see it happening. But no-one says anything. It's just accepted. The way some of the others look at the victims – it's like they all suddenly believe that person *must* deserve it," said Lopez.

"What did they make you do?" said Lucy.

"I was sent with some other grunts to go and loot the enemy's empty hotel. The Queen's guards secured the building, and a bunch of us were sent to go and raid the supplies," said Lopez.

"Why didn't you run – you could've escaped?" said Lucy.

"We were guarded the whole time. But I think we may have an angle on getting out of here. I spoke to Willis," said Lopez.

"The soldier?" said Lucy.

"Yeah, his hand's still fucked, and he's been ostracized. The others are treating him like he's toxic – they don't want anything to do with him. I think he's our way out. We'll approach him tomorrow. Rest up until then, you look like shit," said Lopez.

"So glad you came back," said Lucy, dryly.

"I mean it – you need to regain some strength. Finish the bread, then sleep some more. Tomorrow, when they take us to the hotel, we'll get Willis away from the others and make our escape," said Lopez.

***

Feb 23rd (est.) – It's night-time. Can't get back to sleep. Someone on our level's still working, so at least there's some candlelight I can use. Didn't think I'd ever get this notebook back. Lopez says the Queen gave it to him when Marissa returned to the HQ last night (along with Rangecroft's diary). He's not said anything, but I'm guessing he read both. He might not have had time. He's gone cold again. I probably talked about Rangecroft's notes too much. Dan always said people you serve with become like family. Something sure has flicked a switch in Lopez's buttoned-up head, 'cos he's back to being a jumped up, pompous, army prick. Before curfew he reverted to calling me "Young", and insisting I call him "Major". Spoilers: in an army of two, that's not gonna happen.

We compared lesions again – they're definitely getting worse. This led us on to arguing about where to go from here. He said DC, because he's obsessed with DC. I said Boston, because the only thing we've heard about anyone treating this disease was mention of a doctor in Boston. He accused me of avoiding DC, which is insane – if he's bothered to read this diary he'll know full well that Dan's father's there. Besides, I'm damned if I tell the "Major" about my mother, when I didn't get to tell Dan. I said if he ever wants to make it to DC, then we have to go to Boston first. I think he knows Boston's our only viable option, he just doesn't want to admit it yet.

He had a go at me for the decisions I'd made so far, like the mall thing, and picking up Maurice. So I told him his judgement had gotten everyone at Camp Oscar killed. He took that badly, and we argued some more. I told him he should stick to worrying about the people he'd lost, and I'd worry about mine. He's barely mentioned the fact that I saved his life yesterday. Didn't even ask for details. Thinks we're all square after one hug? Like I said: asshole.

***

A loud bang struck the glass cubicle, shattering Lucy's deep slumber.

"On your feet for the Queen!" bellowed a guard, storming through the corridor, banging a stick against each cubicle as she went.

The pale grey daylight of a winter morning shone in from the windows. Lucy rose to her feet with the others and stumbled out into the corridor, where dozens of other residents were spilling out. People began jostling forwards, vying for a position near the front, where guards held the crowd back with batons. Lucy guessed there were around a hundred people crammed into her corridor, and probably the same on the parallel aisle.

The elevator door opened with a ding and the crowd erupted with cheers. Lucy craned her neck for a view of the Queen, as she stepped out onto the floor and waved to the filthy, stinking residents. A gong sounded, and the crowed fell silent.

"I ask only one thing of you, if you wish to be citizens in the new world I am offering. Loyalty. Be loyal to our vision, be loyal to each other, be loyal to me, and together we will forge a great future.

126

Some of you are new here, and have joined us in the last day or so. To you I say, welcome – you are on the path to citizenship. Others of you may have been here for longer. To you I say, persevere. Your efforts do not go unnoticed, and we are preparing room for you above."

The Queen paused and smiled at the crowd, the foremost rows of whom cheered and applauded enthusiastically, while the rear rows were more cautious. The Queen held up a hand and the applause died down.

"Loyalty and citizenship go hand in hand. If one is strong, so is the other. But we are all human, and we all make mistakes. Sometimes, that can seem like disloyalty, and for some of you, that is why you have found yourselves here. But take heart, for your fate is in your hands. You have the power to prove your commitment, to remold yourself, and to carve out a citizenship of the highest possible order. This morning I bring proof of this very fact. Among you is one who had much to prove. One who had much trust to build. But they have proven themselves a thousand fold. It is thanks to their courage, and their efforts, that we have eliminated the threat from our enemies, and preserved the safety of our community."

Lopez looked at Lucy uneasily.

"I told this person there would be reward if they proved themselves to me, and I am a woman of my word. Today, I am proud to welcome Maurice back into the new order as a fully-fledged citizen," said the Queen.

The crowd cheered as the Canadian stepped forwards from the front row – aided by the guards – and bowed before the Queen.

"To all of you here today, take heart from this. There is redemption for your mistakes, and there is reward for your loyalty. Think what you can achieve today, that might make you a citizen," said the Queen.

She ushered Maurice into the lift, with her guards, and entered after them, waving to the crowd as the door closed.

"Five minutes until roll call, five minutes, back to your quarters," called a guard, dispersing the crowds back inside their glass cubicles.

Lucy and Lopez filed back into their cubicle after the Chinese. A guard shoved a basket of bread across the floor, and two bowls of water, then sealed the door. Two of the Chinese dived for the bread bowl, only to be beaten by the third. Clutching the prize, he handed a piece to each person, including Lucy and Lopez, then divided the remaining pieces into equal strips and shared them out.

Lopez went to wash his face in the water but the same man pulled the bowl away from him.

"What the hell?" said Lopez.

The Chinese man pointed to Lopez's arm, then shook his finger. He repeated the gesture until Lopez conveyed he'd understood. They ate their bread while the other three washed their faces and armpits in the water, then slid the bowl over to Lucy and Lopez, who used the remainder.

The door slid open.

"Well, well, I guess you kids are with me today," said Sergeant Adler, standing the threshold, Taser in hand. His thin lips were cracked in a sinister smile, and his penetrating eyes amplified by his thick glasses. Lucy grabbed her backpack and vacated the cell with the others. They headed downstairs, flanked by the Sergeant.

"Going hiking, Young?" said Adler.

"What?" said Lucy.

"Your bag," said Adler.

"We're looting, right? Gotta carry the stuff in something," said Lucy.

Satisfied by the logic, Adler shrugged and ordered them out into the forecourt. They crossed under the razor wire perimeter and past the bus blockade to the street beyond, where a pickup awaited them. Lucy glanced into the open trunk of the crashed SUV. The father's arm hung limply over the back seat headrest. His skin looked grey and moist. She tore her eyes away and hurried on to the loading area.

Several other groups were also being escorted to trucks and vans. The guards surrounding and driving the vehicles were armed with pistols and rifles. It wasn't until Lucy's group was loaded into the truck that the supervising guard gave Adler a pistol, to accompany his Taser.

As they drove to the hotel, Lucy's eyes were drawn to the oxidizing blood stains in the snow, and the degrading bodies before them. Priestly had been telling the truth.

"The hotel's worse. Just a heads up," said Lopez, following her gaze.

They arrived at the familiar five story hotel with the other trucks. Adler ordered them all off and briefed them on the sidewalk. Lucy's eyes flicked to the parked car opposite – it was the one she'd hidden behind yesterday, before taking the young girl hostage.

"Same drill. Food, drink, drugs, take 'em. If you find a weapon, hand it to one of us immediately. Anything else, make a call. The better you do, the quicker you'll get your citizenship. Alright, get going," said Adler.

Lucy followed Lopez inside. Blood stained the walls and carpets as they traipsed through the lobby, where bodies were in the advanced stages of decomposition. They joined a train of other workers and guards pouring into the stairwell.

"We need to catch Willis's group – go quick," whispered Lopez.

Lucy pushed forwards through the other climbers, barging her way to the front with Lopez close behind.

"This one," she said, peeling off on the third level, after the disappearing Willis.

Lopez followed her onto the corridor, where Willis stood guard among the dozen workers raiding the apartments.

"This ain't your floor," said Willis. His hand was still thickly bandaged.

"Hear us out. I saw you yesterday, I know you don't want to be here. Neither do we. Come with us," said Lopez, lowering his voice and getting close to Willis.

"And go where?" scoffed Willis, through his thick black beard.

"Somewhere you're respected again," said Lopez.

"I'd rather have food than respect," said Willis.

"You used to have both, but your boys have turned on you. You think that's gonna get better? You're the runt," whispered Lopez.

"Shut your fuckin' mouth," said Willis, reaching for his Taser.

"Woah, cool it," said Lucy, raising her hands, as some of the other workers passed by, looking on warily. "Look at your hand.

Your 'friends' stood by and let it happen. Now they're treating you like crap to curry favor with the Queen. You really wanna keep on down that path? To hell with all of them, Willis. Take control again. Break out of here with us," said Lucy.

"Where would we even go?" said Willis.

"South," said Lucy.

Lopez's lip twitched but he held his tongue.

"South?" said Willis.

"Like you planned. There's nothing for us here, or north or west of here, so we wanna go south. We need warmth and food, and I'm reckoning Mexico has both," said Lucy.

"I don't need you two fuckers. If I go, I can make it on my own," said Willis, straightening up.

"Then how come you're still here? You *do* need us, Willis. Think about it – even stealing the car could attract hostiles. The driver needs at least one shooter to cover them. Plus with three of us we could drive almost continuously by taking shifts. We'd only need to stop for fuel. We're your best chance of escape," said Lucy.

"Even if I wanted to help, there are three guards down there, and you two ain't even armed," said Willis.

"We need to do this without guns anyway – if we fire shots, then our escape's blown wide open. This has to be quick and quiet. Give us your Taser," said Lopez.

"Fuck you," said Willis.

"You'll still have your pistol, to use as a club. But us two need *something* to pull this off," said Lopez.

"Willis, if we're gonna do this, it has to be now. The others will start coming down soon. Are you with us or not?" said Lucy.

Willis glanced around the corridor then un-holstered his Taser and handed it to Lucy. "Peters is on duty outside, on the third van. I'll tell him Adler wants him, instead of me," said Willis.

"Will he believe you?" said Lucy.

"He believe anythin' if weakness is the reason," said Willis. He waved his bandaged hand with a grimace.

"OK, so that's one guard down, what about the others?" said Lopez.

"We s'posed to load the front van first. If you two find somethin' to carry it'll give y'all a reason to approach the first driver without lookin' suspicious. Keep the Taser hidden, get the driver to open their door, then stun 'em," said Willis.

"Won't the guard behind hear it?" said Lucy.

"I'll get to him. Follow me," said Willis.

Lucy and Lopez grabbed a duvet and some pillows each so that their arms were filled, then followed Willis downstairs and onto the street. Willis headed for the third van, where Peters sat behind the wheel, smoking.

"Serge wants you upstairs," said Willis, waving at Peters.

"How come?" said Peters, opening the door and puffing out a plume of smoke, his whole face seemingly shrinking as he did so.

"He said something about me being a useless piece of shit," said Willis, waving his bandaged hand.

Peters laughed, and got out.

"He ain't wrong. Hey what are these two doing?" said Peters, spotting Lucy and Lopez.

"The fuck's wrong with you two? I told you, load the front van first," snapped Willis, shoving both Lopez and Lucy down the sidewalk.

"So much for the 'chosen ones'," snorted Peters, heading inside.

Lucy adjusted her grip on the Taser as she approached the front van, shifting the duvet's folds so the tip was poised, ready to fire. She reached the driver's window and stared at the woman behind the wheel, vacantly.

"Put it in the trunk," said the driver, her voice muffled by the glass.

Lucy frowned and stepped closer to the van so that the duvet touched the metalwork. Behind them, she could hear Willis engaging the second van's driver in conversation.

"Jesus, are you two simple or something?" said the woman, opening the van door. "Stick it in the—"

Lucy pulled the trigger and the Taser embedded in the guard's stomach. The woman snapped into a rigid contortion and moaned as the volts coursed through her body.

"Hey!" cried the second guard, but Willis silenced him with a pistol whip.

Major Lopez dropped the bedding and ran to the second guard, grabbing his pistol and Taser, while Lucy disarmed the first driver and hauled her twitching body onto the ground.

"Freeze!" came a cry from the sidewalk.

Lucy spun around, pistol in hand. A guard stood in the threshold to the hotel, registering his two incapacitated colleagues. Lucy recognized him as the father she'd seen on the Queen's couch; the man who'd pledged his services to buy medication for his daughter. Armed, and in a rag-tag uniform, he looked nervous.

"Everything's under control, just be calm, man, there's no need to point that thing at me," said Willis, hiding his pistol behind his back.

"What the hell's going on?" said the father, anxiously.

"Li'l misunderstanding, that's all," said Willis.

"They're escaping?" said the man, his eyes widening with panic.

"No-one's escaping, man, just be calm," said Willis, flicking off the safety catch.

"They can't go – if they go, the Queen will punish us," insisted the father.

"It's cool, man, these two are heading back inside. Would you mind escorting them? I'm s'posed to stay with the vehicles," said Willis.

"Hands in the air – you should all do that," said the father, anxiously.

"My hand is straight-up fucked, man," said Willis.

"Don't screw with me, hands in the air, all of you!" stammered the father.

Lopez raised his hands, revealing the pistol and Taser.

"Drop them," cried the father.

Lopez obliged.

"You too," said the father, pointing at Willis.

"I'm on your side, god dammit," said Willis.

"Then show me your other hand," said the father.

The next second unfolded in slow motion for Lucy. Willis whipped his hand around, training the pistol at the father. But the nervous man was quicker. He fired first, hitting Willis in the shoulder. As Willis fell against the car with a cry, the father took aim at Lopez, but Lucy pulled her trigger, striking the father in the chest. The man collapsed to the ground.

"Go!" cried Lopez, running towards the front van.

Lucy tore her eyes from the father's motionless body and leapt into the driver's seat.

"You assholes, what about me? Hey, yo, help! They're escaping!" cried Willis, reaching for his pistol.

Another shot fired, and Willis fell silent. Lopez leapt into the passenger seat and pulled his seat belt on, pistol in hand, as Lucy hit the gas.

FIVE

Doctor

The van slowed to a halt. Heavy rainfall had cleared Boston's streets of snow, and left the storm drains awash. They were somewhere in the metropolis – neither of them knew the city. They'd slept in the van that night, on the city's outskirts, but the sleep had done nothing to alleviate their hunger. Lucy's stomach churned. Her head felt light. She rubbed her upper arm. The lesions were spreading. Lopez's were worsening too. Both of them knew it but neither said it: they were growing weaker by the day.

The van's fuel was critically low. She always knew tracking the rumored doctor down was going to be a long shot, but only now, as they trawled the deserted streets, did she realize quite how desperate their plan was. For the past twenty minutes, they'd been honing in on two thin smoke plumes – the only hints of life so far.

"Of course," said Lopez, slowing the van to a halt.

The street ahead – tantalizingly close to the grey stacks – was sealed off by overturned cars.

"Next block?" suggested Lucy.

Her optimism was soon dashed. Block after block was sealed off, using a mixture of improvised but heavy-duty barriers made of buses, concrete blocks, shipping containers, and sandbags. They followed the unyielding perimeter for at least a kilometer before it turned sharply and extended in the perpendicular direction. They followed the new stretch until they reached something resembling a checkpoint.

A line of concrete bollards spanned the width of the street like a highway barrier. Towering over them was a wall of sandbags two stories high. Behind that, Lucy guessed there must have been a scaffold platform, because guards were stationed amidst the upper row, staring down at the new arrivals along the barrels of their rifles.

Lopez left the engine running and they waited for a moment, but no greeting party came.

"Shall we do this?" said Lucy, placing her hand on the door.

"I guess if they were gonna shoot us outright, they'd have done it by now," said Lopez.

Together they stepped out onto the damp street, hands raised.

"State your purpose," called a sentry from above.

"We're looking for a doctor," said Lucy.

"Are you infected?" said the sentry.

Lucy glanced at Lopez. "We think so," she replied.

"Then you need to move on," said the sentry.

"We're with the US Army. We need shelter," said Lopez.

"You're in the quarantined zone. No-one from the quarantined zone enters these walls," said the sentry.

"What's behind the walls?" asked Lucy.

"You need to move on now," said the sentry.

"Wait, so we're in the quarantined zone? What else is here?" said Lopez.

"A lot," said the sentry.

"Are there any other military personnel in there with you?" said Lopez.

"Sir, you're not coming in," said the sentry.

"We're the army, for Christ's sake!" protested Lopez.

"No such thing," said the sentry.

"I've been saying that for days," muttered Lucy.

"Look at our uniforms, look at the damned flag. This is insane - we're American soldiers, on American soil, and you're shutting us out?" said Lopez.

"It ain't about being a soldier, or an American. It's about clean or infected. You're the wrong one," said the sentry.

"To hell with that. Who's in charge? I want to speak to whoever runs this place," demanded Lopez.

"Not gonna happen," said the sentry.

"Is it a soldier? A cop? Some politician?" said Lopez.

The sentry said nothing.

"Mother *fucker*!" cried Lopez, slamming his fist on the hood. "I *said* we should've gone to DC."

Lucy ignored Lopez and addressed the scout.

"Please, we just wanna see the doctor," said Lucy.

"She's not here," said the sentry.

"But she's real?" implored Lucy.

"Yuh-huh," said the sentry, with a weary tone.

"You know her?" said Lucy.

"I tried telling her to stay, but she wouldn't hear it. She'd made up her mind – both of them had," said the sentry.

"There's two doctors?" said Lucy.

"Used to be. Only one now. We told them it's what'd happen if they went into the quarantine zone, but they didn't listen. They knew it was a one-way trip," said the sentry.

"Is it true that she's got a cure?" said Lucy.

"How would I know? I'm not sick," said the sentry.

"Where do we find her?" said Lopez, tetchily.

"Look, I haven't seen her in weeks, alright? As far as I know she goes where the sick people go. If you can find more sick people, like, a colony, wait there and she'll find you," said the sentry.

"Where are they?" said Lucy.

"Mostly north side. From what I've heard, it ain't pretty," said the sentry.

"Come on," said Lucy, opening the van door.

Lopez opened the driver's side.

"Hey, where did you guys come from?" called the sentry.

"A lot of places," said Lucy.

"New York," said Lopez.

"So the infection's spread down there?" said the sentry.

"There are worse things there than the infection," said Lucy.

"But how did you get infected?" called the sentry.

"Great fucking question," yelled Lopez, slamming the door.

***

They drove for a few miles, leaving the wall behind as they headed north into the city. Lopez scratched his face and shuffled in his seat, exhaling heavily through flared nostrils. He made a point of examining his black eye in the mirror several times, tutting loudly. As the van spluttered to a halt, having exhausted the last of its gas, he finally snapped.

"This is bullshit," he cried, slapping the steering wheel.

Lucy looked around and considered their options. There was nowhere in sight to refuel.

"It can't be far to the outbreak zone – the sentry said it was several miles and I reckon we've covered a good few since the wall," she suggested.

"Right, cos your judgement is just fuckin' A," said Lopez, getting out and slamming the door.

"Excuse me?" said Lucy, climbing out after him.

"If it wasn't for you, I'd be in DC right now," said Lopez.

"You're saying this is *my* fault?" said Lucy.

"*Everything's* your fault, Young. You're a ruiner. Ever since I found you on that miserable hillbilly backroad you've brought nothing but chaos," said Lopez.

"Really? Then who saved your sorry ass from the Queen? If I hadn't come back, she'd have killed you, remember? Tortured you first," said Lucy.

"It's your fault I was even there! God *dammit* I should've left you at the mall – let that mob of civilians overrun you. No – I should've followed my instincts way before that. I should've ditched you when you fell asleep on one pitiful shift of night watch. But I was *weak* – I felt sorry for you, Young, I wanted to help you. I thought I could show you how to adapt, how to become the soldier you need to be. Boy was I wrong. Worse than that, not only have you failed to become any kind of soldier, but you've killed good soldiers along the way. Dead people, wherever you go. You got Jackson killed. You sent Rangecroft on a suicide mission. Come to think of it, you say you killed all those guys on the farm – you say they attacked you. Was it really that way round? I see a pattern of behavior in you, Young, and I'm wondering how far back the trail goes," said Lopez.

Lucy swallowed as each dead face flashed across her mind. The harder she tried to dismiss them, the more vivid their memories became. The father she'd shot in New York, Jackson, Whitaker, Rangecroft, Kerman's gang, the boy, the survivors from the train wreck, Dan –

Nausea swept over her. There was a ringing in her ears. Lopez was shouting at her, but his words were a blur. She slumped against the van and cradled her head as he ranted.

"Are you even listening to me? Christ!" he proclaimed, slamming the hood again, making Lucy start.

She scrambled to her feet and stared at him, her eyes wild. Lopez looked gaunt. The skin on his face was becoming blotchy – the first signs of fresh lesions.

"Are you even going to defend yourself? Do you even care?" demanded Lopez.

"Of course I care!" yelled Lucy, fuming. "I *saved* Jackson, I gave her the–"

"Powder, right. That god damned *poison* you made us eat. Every damned situation, you make things worse. It almost seems willful. Have you gone off people, is that it?" said Lopez.

Lucy's fists clenched.

"Maybe if you'd spent four months–" began Lucy.

141

"Christ, Young, it really is all about you, isn't it? Is your selfishness just genetic, or did you choose to be this way?" said Lopez.

Lucy swallowed as memories of her father and mother clashed in her mind.

"My mom's somewhere in this city. If we find her, you can ask her yourself," she snapped.

"Your mom's here? Of course she is. *Of course she is*. It couldn't have just been about getting the cure, oh no – because we could almost *certainly* have gotten that in DC. But hey, why bother telling me before we set off? Christ, it's like everything you do is designed to shit on the people around you," growled Lopez.

"That is *so* unfair. If it wasn't for me, you'd be dead already. I could've run – on that first mission for the Queen, you know? I could've abandoned you and saved myself, but no, I came back for you. *I come back for people*," said Lucy, spitting.

"You came back because you *owed* me, Young. You rescuing that sniveling Canadian – *against* my orders – is the whole reason we ended up in that insanity. I've seen what you do to the people around you, and it sure isn't help them. The only thing you care about is wiping the blood off your hands. If only I'd let that mob take you, Jackson would still be alive. Or maybe I should've carried on running in that forest. Why in *hell's* name I surrendered to save *you*, I'll never know," said Lopez.

"I helped Jackson. I helped both of you," fumed Lucy, her muscles tensing as Dan's face clawed at her mind.

"Bullshit! You're a *curse*, Young, and one of these days, you're gonna have to explain why it is that *everyone* around you seems to die," shouted Lopez.

Lucy screamed and threw herself at Lopez, catching him off guard. She tackled him to the ground and pounded him with her fists; kneeing him, kicking, tearing at his hair as the rage poured out of her. Lopez fought off her pummeling and rolled her off, tussling for control.

"You murdering piece of shit," grunted Lopez, pinning her down. He clamped her between his legs and grabbed her throat with both hands.

"*Liar*," choked Lucy, grabbing his hair and pulling with all her might.

She tore out a clump. As Lopez howled, his grip slackened just enough for Lucy to capitalize. She seized his right hand and bit down hard. With his left hand he punched her in the ribs. Lucy gasped, unclenching her jaw. Lopez snatched his bitten hand away. He punched her hard in the face, striking her right eye and causing her vision to blur. She stared at the blue sky overhead and felt a sense of tranquility, as Lopez's silhouette loomed over her once again, his fist balled up, ready to strike.

Lucy felt his legs slacken. The vice-like grip binding her eased and Lopez slumped to the ground. Lucy disentangled herself from him and crawled to her knees. He was unconscious. She panted, catching her breath, as she scrambled away from him. She rose to her knees, but as she reached for her gun, a dizziness swept over her. As she collapsed to the ground, the last thing she saw was Lopez's face, pressed into the tar.

***

Lucy blinked her eyes open. She was in someone's lounge. It was tidy. Sunlight peeked through the drawn curtains. The sound of metal on metal drew her attention to the far corner, where a man sat, sharpening a knife. Lucy flinched, expecting to have to fight to free herself – but her hands were unbound.

"Oh, you're up," said the man, setting the knife down and standing up. His tone was flat. He wore a deep violet boiler suit, covered in oily stains. The suit was padded in an uneven fashion by layers of clothing beneath. The man was around forty. He had a short grey beard. Bags hung under his eyes, and his cheeks were thin.

Lucy recoiled, drawing her legs towards her. She was on a brown leather couch. It felt soft, and squeaked as she moved.

"That's gonna come up like a peach," said the man, pointing towards her fat eye.

The man's eyelids hung low, his expression a mixture of weariness and cynicism.

"Where's Lopez?" said Lucy.

"Your friend? In the guest room. He looked worse than you so I put him on the bed," said the man

"Who are you?" said Lucy.

"Jay," said the man.

Lucy nodded, as if that had answered the question.

"Did you bring us here?" she asked.

"I found you both passed out on the street. Couldn't just leave you there – not safe," said Jay, shaking his head.

"Is this your house?" said Lucy.

"One of them. You had the good fortune to pass out on my corner. Which is lucky, because I couldn't have dragged you much more. I get weak, like you," said the man, pulling his collar down to reveal lesions across his neck.

"Why did you help us?" said Lucy,

"Us folk gotta stick together," said Jay.

He fetched a sports bottle from the counter.

"Thirsty?" he said, holding it out for Lucy.

She eyed the bottle up.

"It's water," he added, taking a demonstrative sip.

Lucy accepted the bottle gratefully and swigged from it. It tasted faintly salty.

"Is this seawater?" said Lucy.

"Freshly desalinated. The store was out of sparkling," said Jay.

Lopez entered from the adjacent room, squinting like a teenager awaking reluctantly on a Monday morning.

"Hey, everyone's up, how about that," said Jay, clapping his hands.

"Who the fuck are you?" said Lopez, leaning against the doorframe, massaging his back. ·

"He's Jay, he's infected," said Lucy.

"What's up," said Jay.

"How long was I out?" said Lopez.

"Couple of hours," said Jay.

"We need to find the doctor – can you take us to her?" said Lucy.

"That's not really how it works. She comes to us. There's a group not far from here. You can wait with them. She's due to visit. Do you guys feel up to moving again?"

Lucy rose to her feet and waited for her head to settle, then nodded.

"How far?" said Lopez.

"Couple of miles, but we gotta move discreetly. If I say freeze, you guys freeze. If I say hide, you hide. You got me?" said Jay.

"I can do that. It's her you should worry about," said Lopez.

Lucy took another swig of the salty water then passed it to Lopez without looking at him. He scoffed, but took it and drank. Lucy checked her holster – she still had her pistol. She grabbed her backpack from the side of the couch, while Jay slung an air rifle over his shoulder.

***

They kept close to Jay as he led them through the suburbs, beneath the clear sky and the faint warmth of the spring sun. He took them on a circuitous route, never staying on one street for more than a few blocks. He checked every junction they reached, and looked behind often.

Lucy studied the name of every passing street, checking to see if it was her mother's. Part of her was hoping her mother's home was buried deep within the walled community – sheltered from the 'quarantine zone' – but she knew this was impossible; the zone was in the south and her mom lived somewhere in the north of the city. She couldn't remember the exact district, but she knew the street name. As they traipsed through the unfamiliar city, Lucy felt a continuous anxiety she might be passing it by, leading to numerous false dawns. The repeated disappointment was, at least, tempered by the desolation of the streets themselves. Broken windows, unkempt drives, strewn litter. She wanted desperately to abandon the mission, pinpoint her mom and go straight there to pour out her soul, forgive the wretched woman and feel loved again. But she needed the medication. If she lost the doctor now, when she was so close, who knows if she'd ever find her again? So Lucy bit her lip and stayed focused on the immediate goal, once again suppressing the wrenching desire to connect with the last of her family.

"You see that?" said Lopez, after a mile's walking.

She followed his gaze to a side street. The corner building had a large black cross painted at eye level – as did the building across from it.

"That's bad news," said Jay, with a grim look. He swiveled his rifle into position, took off the safety, and moved towards the street.

"We're going in?" said Lucy.

"Be ready," said Jay.

"For what?" hissed Lopez, drawing his pistol.

Lucy eyed up the buildings around them. *Clifford Street,* read the sign. A couple of homes had barricaded windows, a few others were smashed. Most had their curtains drawn. The houses were beautiful – quaint, old-fashioned detached buildings – but the vandalism and ragged lawns, covered in rotting leaves and fallen branches, confirmed their desertion.

Jay stopped moving. He held his fist up to the others to copy. Lucy peered around him at the hold up. Ahead to the right, a large house had a stone wall at the boundary between its garden and the sidewalk. The wall was around two feet high, and had a hedgerow growing above it. But the wall was broken; several sections of it had been pulverized and lay in ruin, with shards of rubble spewing onto the sidewalk.

"Oh my God," said Lopez, drawing her attention to the house directly opposite the wall.

Lucy's stomach churned. Tied to a lamppost was the body of a man. His faced was pulverized and bloody, as were his chest and limbs. All around him lay large, jagged stones the size of bricks. Hung around his battered neck was a wooden board with one word written across it in large, black capitals: *SINNER*.

"What happened?" said Lucy, queasily.

"The Faithful. They think our disease is a punishment from God. They call this 'absolution'," said Jay, gesturing to the rocks.

"We should get away from here – the creatures will track it by nightfall," said Lucy.

"What creatures?" said Jay, giving Lucy a puzzled look.

"The beasts – whatever you call them. We don't wanna be around when they turn up. We don't know enough about this 'immunity' to rely on it, especially when we're getting weaker," said Lucy.

"You lost me," said Jay.

"Wait, you really don't have beasts here?" said Lucy, in astonishment.

"We have the Faithful. You could call them that," said Jay.

"Who are they?" said Lopez.

"They're the biggest group of survivors in Boston," said Jay.

"You're telling me the survivors in this city want to be part of a group that does that?" said Lucy, gesturing to the mutilated bodies.

"Believe it or not, in many ways they're an improvement on their predecessors. Everyone flocked to them when they outlawed the unspeakables," said Jay.

"The 'unspeakables'?" said Lucy.

"Jeez, you guys really don't know anything, huh?" said Jay.

"TripAdvisor was down when we set off," said Lopez, without smiling.

"The virus wiped out most of the city, and after that there was just chaos. No law, no order. There were just groups of survivors stealing, fighting, and looting from each other, and that's how winter started. The supplies left across the city began to run out, and we'd already eaten all the dogs and rodents. There was only one source of meat left," said Jay.

"Jesus Christ," said Lopez, gravely.

"No-one wanted it. It started out as just eating those who had passed naturally – while they were still safe to eat. But that's a difficult window; to find a recently-deceased body *and* do so before anyone else. So people started killing the weakest people for food. In the first weeks, a lot of folk refused to be part of it – but their abstinence only made them weaker, while the unspeakables grew stronger. The stronger they got, the bolder they became, and they started hunting more openly. Groups of hunters soon turned into tribes, as people rushed to join them before they fell victim. Of course, once the limited supply of weak humans had been eaten, there were only strong, hungry cannibals left roaming the city. So the cannibals turned on each other, attacking rival tribes, and preying on the weakest in their own packs. The tribes began to collapse, and that's when the Faithful arrived – bringing grain supplies for survivors, and 'eradicating the scourge of the unspeakables'," said Jay.

"So they're not from Boston?" said Lucy.

"From what I've heard, the leader was a farmer from out of town. His grain stores supported the community through winter, and people became loyal to him because of it – seeking him out, even. He and his followers heard what was happening in Boston and decided it was their divine mission to purge the city of sin," said Jay.

"So other survivors in Boston converted to the Faithful?" said Lucy.

"Very quickly – once word got out that the newcomers had grain and weren't gonna eat you, well, the case for joining sold itself," said Jay.

"Except that they're barbarians," said Lopez, pointing to the bloodied corpses.

"It's all relative. As long as you're not the one being stoned, then what's not to like?" said Jay, grimacing.

"Were you in a tribe?" said Lucy, warily.

"Jeez guys, *I'm* not gonna eat you – we're on the same side," said Jay.

"This group – the 'Faithful' – can no-one stop them?" said Lopez.

"Why would anyone stop them? Most people *are* them. The only other two communities big enough to take them on don't want to – those pious hypochondriac assholes behind the wall don't care about anyone outside the wall, and the police have barricaded them and theirs inside a prison, so there's no reaching them either. Both sides know we're being hunted, and they don't care."

"Cowards. No honor," spat Lopez.

"Meh, I get it. What's worse, some people stoning a leper to death, or catching leprosy yourself? They're all scared of the disease, see, and if a homicidal religious group happens to spring up and eradicate the outbreak before springtime, then isn't that just swell? Of course, I personally don't wish to be eradicated, so thank god for the doctor. If she can keep us going long enough to figure out a cure, we'll have a community of our own. We're getting stronger with treatment, bit by bit. Speaking of, we should keep moving," said Jay, glancing around and setting off at a brisk pace.

"How did you get infected?" said Lucy, marching to keep up.

"No idea. I woke up one day with weird marks on my skin and the group freaked. They kicked me out," said Jay.

"How many people were in your group?" said Lopez.

"A dozen. I reckon there are a lot of small groups like that across the city – friends that laid low through winter, played it smart. How did you guys get infected?" said Jay.

"Why don't you tell him, Young? Tell Jay how we got infected," said Lopez.

They traipsed on for several more yards.

"We made a mistake," said Lucy, staring at the ground.

***

It was another mile before they reached the safe house. Jay peeled off onto a street that looked indistinguishable from the others. More boarded up windows and overturned trash cans. Jay led them through the yard of a detached house, and down the side passage into the back garden. He delivered a coded knock upon the door.

A finger pulled back the blind and an eye peeped out. Jay waved. The blind fell back into place and the door opened.

"Who they?" demanded the woman.

"They're like us," said Jay, stepping into the kitchen.

"You mean hungry?" said the diminutive woman, sternly. Her eyebrows were painted on, and she wore large hoop earrings.

"I've brought food," said Jay.

"Mmm-hmm," said the woman, watching as Jay swiveled off his backpack and pulled out a stack of large, damp-looking leaves.

"Again?" said the woman.

"Ada, There was nothing else," said Jay.

"You guys eat that?" said Lopez.

"What even is it?" said Lucy.

"No idea. One of our group found we could eat them, though, and they've done us alright since then. If you know which trees to look for, they're not too hard to find," said Jay.

The kitchen was only marginally warmer than outside. A dozen people sat around on chairs, eyeballing the new arrivals.

"I'mma plate up, we feeding the outsiders too?" said Ada, doing little to hide her contempt.

"They're not outsiders, Dee, they're like us," said Jay.

The woman mumbled as she tore the leaves up in a large mixing bowl, then distributed them among smaller plates and bowls which the onlookers received readily. Some members were too weak to feed themselves, so others ground their portions into a paste and spoon-fed them. Lucy leaned against the counter awkwardly. Lopez walked pointedly to the far side of the room and hovered by the defunct fridge.

"No sign of the doc?" said Jay, chewing.

"She came. We all cured," said Ada.

Another resident snorted.

"You gonna eat that?" said a lesion-covered man, leaning towards Lucy's untouched plate.

"Uh, I think so, yeah," said Lucy.

She pinched a bunch of leaves together. They were soggy, and deeply unappetizing, but she was starving. She pressed them into her mouth, catching the juice as it dribbled down her chin. She winced as she chewed. The taste was pungent and vinegary, but not unpalatable.

"All done," said the woman with painted eyebrows, licking her bowl clean.

"Then someone better get more," said Jay.

"I ain't going nowhere. Not in my condition. Your stranger folk look like they can still walk, though," said Ada, pointing at Lucy and Lopez. "How's about they earn their keep."

***

Feb 27th (est.) - It's been two days since we arrived at the sick house. No sign of the doc. One person died yesterday. Others are looking weaker. Lopez looks like hell, and is barely talking to me. He's still mad we're not in DC, and mad that he's infected at all. It doesn't seem to have occurred to him that I'm in the exact same boat.

We've slept almost continuously since arriving here. I dreamt about Dan again. I dreamt we were in San Francisco, heading out on a date. It was bliss. I'd say waking up is the most depressing part of the day, but that would be a disservice to the rest of the day. The first two or three seconds of the day are pristine – my brain is slow, and for the briefest of moments, I'm awake, but I've forgotten everything. It's like I've got him again. Then I remember he's dead, and every day it breaks me a little more. The second thing I remember is that I'm dying of an unknown disease. And the third is that I might not get to see mom before it happens.

The community here is pretty bleak. It's a house full of sick, dying, hungry people, most of whom are mourning their loved ones who either died before them or, worse, sent them into exile. We all share the same room to keep the warmth up, and each stay wrapped in five or more layers of clothes. People only wake up to eat more leaves, which seem to grow all around the area. Jay took me and Lopez to gather some yesterday. He showed us where to look and which ones to take. It's gotta be the big ones – the smaller ones are poisonous, apparently. A different man left this morning to get more food but he's not returned.

I'm feeling weaker. It's getting harder to think. My skin is sore, and the lesions are covering almost the entirety of my back and arms now. I'm dizzy much of the time.

Today I tried to tell Lopez more about my mom – sorry, my estranged *mom – and how the agency tracked her down to Boston. Telling him like that, well, it wasn't how I thought the conversation would go. It wasn't a conversation. That would've required him to speak. I'm trapped, and my only real company is socially incapacitated by his own denial about the collapse of his precious army. Jay listened, at least. He told me where Mom's street is. It's across town, around six miles from here. If I ever regain strength, I will go. If I don't, I wonder if she'll ever know how close I got.*

Heaven knows what Dan would have said. I should've told him about Mom. I was going to. I never thought he'd be stolen from me. But here we are. Five months on and now I'm the one dying. Maybe we'll meet on the other side.

We won't though, will we? It would just be another lie to tell myself. If I believed in another side, I'd be there already. But I don't. And neither did he. Which breaks my heart, because the closer to death I get, the closer time gets to forgetting him.

***

The kitchen door crashed open, waking Lucy abruptly.

"She needs help!" cried Ada, her eyes wide and her painted eyebrows arched in earnest.

Lucy staggered to her feet, swaying as she rose.

Jay sprang to the doorway and bent down, scooping under the newcomer's arms. He dragged her fully into the kitchen while Ada resealed the door.

"Does anyone know first aid?" cried Jay.

Lopez stumbled towards the incapacitated stranger – a woman.

"Stop the bleeding," mumbled the newcomer, clutching her arm.

"Get her coat off – we need to bandage the wound," said Lopez, steadying himself against the counter. His speech was slurred, and his usually warm-bronze skin ghostly pale.

Jay fought the woman's zip, freeing her from the thick coat. The lining was shiny and wet with blood. Others residents appeared with tea towels and rags for bandages. The newcomer's shirt sleeve was torn across her upper arm, where her skin and muscle had been ripped apart by a bullet. Her wound was raw, and the flesh contoured. Blood oozed between the woman's fingers as she tried to clamp the bleeding.

Lopez knelt down to tie the bandage but his fingers were trembling.

"Shit. You gotta do it," said Lopez.

"Me?" said Jay, aghast.

"You're strongest here. Tie the damned knot as hard as you can," slurred Lopez.

Jay obliged, wrapping the bandage around the wound as tightly as he could, and tying the knot hard like a boot lace. He knelt back and watched as blood continued to seep from the wound.

"It's not gonna work – we need a tourniquet," said Lopez.

He grabbed a long wooden spoon from the counter.

"Tie another bandage above the wound – high, near her shoulder. Do the first part of your knot then stop," said Lopez, his eyelids dipping.

Jay obliged, clamping the upper-most part of the woman's arm with a tea towel and crossing the material over itself once, firmly. Lopez knelt down and place the wooden spoon over the center of the knot.

"Use the ends to tie a second knot over the spoon," said Lopez.

Jay did, so, securing the center of the spoon handle, smearing the light wood with blood as his hands worked.

"Now twist it around," said Lopez.

Jay twirled the spoon around like the needle on a compass. The woman moaned in pain.

"More – it's gotta be tighter," grunted Lopez.

Jay wound it around several times more – causing the woman's arm to bulge under the pressure, as twists of fabric wound themselves beneath the spoon and crushed her arm. She pounded the floor with her free arm, as the agony only increased.

"That's enough – now hold it steady," slurred Lopez.

He took a rag and tied it above the tourniquet, pulling it as tight as his trembling fingers could manage, into a firm double-knot.

"Under there," said Lopez.

Jay tucked the thin end of the spoon under Lopez's knot and released it. The tourniquet held. The stream of crimson subsided.

"Someone write the time down. We need to try and release the pressure in increments. Fifteen minute intervals," said Lopez, pointing to the kitchen clock.

"Who is she?" whispered Lucy, to a fellow resident.

"Charlie," he replied without taking his eyes off the blood-soaked woman on the floor, "She's the doctor. She's all we got."

***

Jay rummaged through the doctor's backpack and retrieved a packet of tablets, which was met with feeble cries of relief. He distributed them among the group. Each resident swallowed eagerly, then returned to their sleeping. He reached Lucy last.

"What are these?" said Lucy, struggling to focus on the pill in her cupped hands.

"They're what you need. This dose will last you a few days, then you take another. That's how it goes," said Jay, stowing the excess tablets in his deep violet, oil-stained boiler suit.

"Yeah but what *is* it?" said Lucy.

"I don't know, read the label," said Jay, handing her the bottle.

"This is chemotherapy," she said, translating the drug's pharmacological name.

"If you say so. You should sleep now – they work best if you sleep right away. Your boy's got the memo," said Jay, gesturing to Lopez, who was out cold.

"He's not my boy," muttered Lucy.

"He tells it different," said Jay, his eyelids heavy, and his expression as deadpan as ever.

Lucy was about to correct him and defiantly explain that Dan was her 'boy', but she couldn't bring herself to say it. The words felt hollow. She thought the crippling loneliness she'd endured over the winter would abate now that she was with people again, but these people didn't know her, and their unfamiliarity was an amplifier for her darkest sorrows.

Jay clearly sensed the question had caused some trouble, and moved the conversation on, albeit without mustering an alternative expression or tone.

"So the doc's stable – for now," he said.

"Right, uh, that's good," said Lucy, swiftly dabbing her eyes dry on her blanket.

"The tourniquet's off but she's still lost a lot of blood. I'll keep an eye on her. Your b- *the Major* told me what to watch for," said Jay.

"Great. Thanks again for the meds," said Lucy.

"Sleep. You need it. I'll catch you on the flipside," said Jay.

Lucy pulled the duvet around her while Jay set about mopping up the doctor's blood. She wanted to grab him, shake him, make him understand. She *had* a boy. She had *Dan*. Her soul mate. But he was gone.

***

"Quit eavesdropping and go do your damned homework," her dad yelled, pressing the phone into his shoulder.

Lucy scarpered back to her room with a "Sorrrrryyyyyy!" and slammed the door with flare. She immediately crouched down, below the handle, and cracked the door ajar again – just wide enough to hear her father's voice.

"Apologies, that was my daughter. Carry on," he said, into the phone. Lucy watched him pace around the kitchen table, in and out of sight of the doorway. "Whaddya mean not covered?" he growled. Lucy cracked the door a little wider. "I know it's expiring, that's why I'm calling you to renew," he said, jabbing the air with his finger.

"How is it a pre-existing condition? Last week I didn't have it, this week I do. I don't see how that- Yeah, no kidding they're expensive, that's why you- To hell with that! Oh, you think? We'll see about that – I wanna speak with your supervisor," he barked.

He vanished from the doorway. Lucy listened as a cupboard door opened, and a glass clinked onto the table. A bottle was unscrewed, and liquid poured.

"Yeah, speaking. Your operative's telling me I'm all of a sudden 'ineligible', and I fail to see what- No, I haven't read that particular- And you expect me to pay for that how? Exactly! Oh, sure, you're positively heartbroken, I can tell. God *dammit* you people are the worst! Oh I'm sorry if my language is colorful, but *fuck. You.* I'll have to sell everything because of this. Everything!" he growled, slamming his glass down on the table.

Her father looked up and made eye contact with Lucy, who gasped, spotted. She tumbled backwards into her room, pulling the door shut and closing her eyes, bracing for the inevitable barrage of parenting.

"God *dammit* girl, what did I tell you about eavesdropping!" he cried.

She darted to the window and swung her feet onto the ledge, dangling her legs over the side. The sea air was bracing. She looked into the dark waters, as waves crashed against the rocks fifty feet below. Her sandal fell off and tumbled downwards, vanishing into the turbulent ocean. A slick of yellow spores bobbed across the rolling water's surface, and extended right out to the horizon.

"Hey, missy!" growled her father, bursting into the bedroom.

Lucy gasped and slipped from the ledge, plunging towards the foaming mass below.

***

The dream had recurred several times since Lucy took the first tablet. Even now, it was occupying her conscious thoughts as she escorted the doctor across the city. It was four days since Charlie's bloody entry into the safe house, and two days since they'd cauterized her wound. That the doctor was even walking such distances was nothing short of a miracle, although she'd been well fed for the mission. It had become clear early on that Charlie couldn't stomach the residents' diet of leaves, so Jay had scavenged some tinned gnocchi for her. Lucy suspected he had a secret stash, but he refuted this.

Yesterday Charlie had insisted she needed to move on. She was nowhere near recovered enough, but she'd been adamant – there were people depending on her. Of course, there were complications. She was weakened and unarmed, having lost her gun during her last encounter with the Faithful. The residents immediately looked to Lucy and Lopez, as soldiers, to step up.

Neither wanted to escort her. Lucy wanted to find her mother, Lopez wanted to get to DC. But neither wanted to donate their weapon to another resident, either, and they owed the doctor their lives. Thus, a deal was struck. While Charlie was in a weakened state, they were to escort her across the city so that she could continue her distribution rounds to the other diseased communities. Lucy's hope was that Charlie would be recovered enough within a week or two to go solo again, or better still they would find suitable replacements to protect her. There was one key return for Lucy and Lopez: extra medication. The doctor knew where to find the remaining drug stockpiles across the city. Not only would the pair get regular treatments without delay, but Lucy and Lopez each stood to amass a personal stockpile.

That was a strong incentive. After just two tablets Lucy looked and felt completely revitalized. The pills had worked quickly and her lesions had vanished. Her strength and focus had been restored – further bolstered by regular leaf meals. She had even grown used to the taste of the putrefied leaves, which were proving to be an incredible source of energy.

Lopez's resentment of Lucy, however, remained palpable, contrary to Jay's interference. The Major's favorite hobby during break periods was to loudly recalculate the distance to DC, and the route he would take there alone. Lucy ignored him, and chose to focus on Charlie. She pressed the doctor for every detail she could glean on the disease, and the cures she'd been trying.

"The drugs work fast, but they wear off fast, too. That's the problem I'm trying to fix – find a longer-acting solution, or at least a way of producing more of them. At the moment, I'm raiding hospitals and pharmacies, and trying to recreate some in my lab, too, but I'm woefully short of test subjects," said Charlie, as they crept through the suburbs.

"You've got a lab, then?" said Lucy, optimistically.

"Sorta. The Faithful trashed my actual lab at MIT, so I've been working in one my friend used to run. It's a small, private outfit, so no-one really knows it's there," explained Charlie.

"How did you know to use chemo?" asked Lucy.

"It kinda made sense. I threw a few samples under the microscope and saw the sort of rapid cell division you'd expect in a cancer. So mitotic inhibitors made sense," said Charlie.

"But they're not a cure?"

"No, it's a band aid," said Charlie

"What happens when they run out?" said Lucy.

"Then you'll wanna be in DC. Because they'll have a cure," grumbled Lopez, chipping in.

"Assuming they're working on it all. Even then, it could take decades to find an actual cure," said Charlie.

"I'll take those odds," said Lopez.

"He's obsessed with DC. Talks of it like it's the freakin' promised land," said Lucy, still astonished at the way Lopez's bitterness was festering.

"The only way we will *ever* climb out of this cesspit of a situation is through a coordinated, technologized effort, and that requires a centralized military operation," Lopez snapped.

"He's not wrong," said Charlie.

"I'm not saying he's wrong, I'm just saying he's being an asshole about being right. Either way, he's a god damned hypocrite," said Lucy.

"*I'm* the hypocrite?" said Lopez.

"Yeah, you are. The guy who professes to be all about the army, and all about reclaiming the nation, and yet who turned his back on every civilian we met since the ambush. You're only helping Charlie now because you need the meds," said Lucy.

"This is rich, coming from the woman whose rescue missions kill more people than they save," said Lopez.

"Can we not do this right now?" said Charlie.

"Fine by me," snapped Lucy.

"Whatever. Let's say you're right, doc, and it takes DC ten years to find that cure. Do we have a decade of chemo drugs lying around?" said Lopez.

"I doubt it. Not the right type, at least," said Charlie.

"So we're screwed," said Lopez.

"Technically mitotic inhibitors are plant alkaloids, so there's a *very* outside chance we could grow long-term treatments for this disease. Assuming no-one kills us firsts," said Charlie.

"You say 'us' like you're infected too," Lopez noted.

"I say it like we're all human," snapped Charlie, bristling.

"Don't get me wrong, it's a good thing," added Lopez.

"That really came across," snarked Lucy.

"I wish everyone shared our views about humanity, Major. The people I left behind the wall are deeply protectionist. I've ostracized myself for this cause," said Charlie.

"Was it hard, leaving your community behind?" said Lucy.

"Of course. We'd made it through so much. We'd survived the virus, survived the unspeakables, and survived the winter – spring was coming. Then we heard of this new disease plaguing the small survivor communities outside the wall, and I knew we had to help. I had to do what was right. If you can't follow your conscience, what hope is there for any of us?" said Charlie.

"Sounds like your wall friends have a different definition of 'conscience'," said Lopez.

"Which is why we left. 'We' – it's just me now, isn't it. Funny how life goes," said Charlie, bitterly.

"I feel you there," said Lucy.

"Ditto that," said Lopez, to Lucy's surprise.

"How many people have you treated?" said Lucy, probing Charlie further.

"Going on eighty," replied the doctor.

"I'm glad to be in that number. We saw a couple die of this thing. Didn't look good," said Lopez.

"It's not the dying you want to worry about. It's the timing. If things go against you, there can be real complications," said Charlie.

"Like what?" said Lucy.

"Like the complete degradation of the human abdomen and bowel," said Charlie.

"For real?" said Lucy, horrified.

"That's kinda what those Faithful people do to you anyway," said Lopez, shrugging.

"How many people have *they* killed?" said Lucy.

"They've only started hunting sufferers recently. Now that the unspeakables are gone, or hiding among other communities, the

Faithful need a new hobby. A new 'righteous cause'. But they don't yet have the resources to purge a whole city, so they do random patrols and raids. They usually catch people foraging for food," said Charlie.

"So there are sick people hiding all over?" said Lopez.

"Yeah, but I can't figure out if that's because the disease is everywhere, or just if it's because people are moving around a lot to evade detection. I've been trying to plot a map of the outbreak but it's proving near impossible to establish a common vector. That's a point – I've yet to take your medical history," said Charlie.

"This again," snorted Lopez.

"What?" said Charlie.

"Ask my executioner," said Lopez, bitterly.

"Screw you," said Lucy.

"Can one of you fill me in?" said Charlie.

"We ingested some white powder," said Lucy, wearily.

Charlie looked baffled.

"It's a toxin that grows off infected D4 creatures. It's poisonous to them, so we took it as a deterrent, so we could escape them. But apparently it's poisonous to us, too," said Lucy.

"Thanks again for the death sentence," said Lopez.

"What were you escaping?" said Charlie.

"The beasts. Jay said you've not had any up here?" said Lucy.

"Not yet," interjected Lopez.

"Is that what 'D4' is?" said Charlie.

"It's one version. Remember the 'virus' that wiped everyone out? Well, it carried on evolving. The bacterium appropriated the DNA of everything it encountered, and one of the end products was a pack predator with enough strength and coordination to threaten the remaining humans across the east coast and the central states. Hell, they reached New York," said Lucy.

"They've made it all the way from the West Coast to New York, but not Boston?" said Charlie.

"Right. So I'm thinking there must be something stopping them?" said Lucy.

"Rivers," said Lopez.

"What?" said Lucy.

"There are rivers that cut across the whole state. I've been thinking about it, planning my route. Say a river's contaminated upstream with a big dose of white powder. That would be a barrier to migrating beasts. Like a line in the sand. Contaminated water could also be what's hitting people round here. Just a theory," he shrugged.

"And you didn't think to share it sooner?" said Lucy.

"I was gonna tell them in DC," said Lopez.

"Hey, we've made it. The safe house is down he-," began Charlie.

She stopped in her tracks. Two bodies sat in the front yard, each tied to a fence post hammered into the center of the lawn. Both corpses were bloodied, and surrounded by rocks. The left corpse had lesions. They each bore a different sign around their neck. The first read *SINNER*, the second, *AGENT OF SATAN*. Charlie knelt down and reached out to the dead man's boot. She dipped her head and sobbed. Lopez placed a consoling hand on her shoulder. After a moment, the doctor drew a sharp breath and stood up, wiping her cheeks.

"This is what they did to Petrov – my lab partner," said Charlie.

Shouts echoed out from the neighboring street. There was the sound of an old-fashioned, hand-held bell ringing. People were shouting aggressively. Their curses and orders were punctuated by an individual's cries for help.

"What's that?" whispered Lucy.

"That's them," said Charlie, anxiously adjusting her sling.

"The people who did this?" said Lopez, gesturing to the corpses.

"Without a doubt," said Charlie.

"You two take shelter – get back to the safe house, I'll find you there," said Lopez.

"What are you doing?" hissed Lucy.

"Protecting the civilians," said Lopez.

"Are you insane? *Now* you're taking a stand? We can't risk them getting Charlie!" said Lucy.

"Which is why you're in charge of her," said Lopez.

"While you do what?" said Lucy.

"You were right, OK? I can't wait for DC to come to them. Not when they're stoning unarmed civilians in the streets. I've *got* a conscience, and I'm saying no more. *I'm* DC," said Lopez.

"Major, if you try this alone-" protested Lucy.

"Get the doc to the safe house," said Lopez, cutting her off.

"I'm not letting you do this. It's a suicide mission," said Lucy. She grabbed Lopez's arm but he shook her off.

"Major, you *can't* leave!" insisted Lucy.

The bell rang out again, prompting more shouts. The cries were getting closer. Somewhere in the maelstrom was an engine.

"For the last time, Young, get inside!" hissed Lopez, shoving her away.

A man careered around the corner, at the far end of their street. He was running, but with a limp. His pant leg was torn, and his leg bloody. The skin on his face was pockmarked with lesions. He spotted Lucy's group and cried out in despair, opening his arms imploringly. A dog bounded across the road and sunk its teeth into the man's calf, dragging him to the ground. Its masters were close behind, their shouts egging the dog on.

"Get down!" hissed Lopez.

The three of them dived behind a car. Lopez took the safety off his pistol and peered around the side. Lucy copied. One of the attacking humans whistled and the dog's snarling ceased instantly. The dog released its ward but stayed looming over him, ready to bite again if instructed. The man lay on his back and begged for mercy, as four humans closed in. Each wore a full length black robe, with the hood pulled up.

A car pulled up by the group. The driver climbed out and kicked the sickly man repeatedly, shouting as he did so. He demanded repentance, and pointed to the car. In the front passenger seat sat a man wearing a robe of brilliant white. Around his neck hung a bronze medallion on a crimson cord. He watched the proceedings without dispassion.

"That's him – the Preacher. He's the cult leader, the one who started it all," gasped Charlie.

"You two get inside the safe house. Stay low. I'm gonna move up and pick as many of them off as I can," whispered Lopez.

"Don't be insane," hissed Lucy.

"If I don't try, then it's all been for nothing," said Lopez.

"What are you talking about! Major, get a grip!" said Lucy.

"It's over, Lucy. You heard the doc. No cure, no drugs, not time left. This is gonna end one way or another. I'm choosing to end this as a soldier," said Lopez.

"Lopez, listen to me, I was *wrong*! You take them on and you'll die. You might kill two of them before they get you, but what difference will it make? We need to get to DC, tell them everything we know, and bring the full weight of justice upon these people. You *cannot* do this alone," insisted Lucy.

"No, no you don't understand. Lucy, this is our chance to kill the Preacher. He's almost never out of the compound, we *have* to try," said Charlie, grabbing Lucy's arm.

"Lopez, don't do this – don't go," implored Lucy.

Lopez stared at her, his eyes narrow, his jaw clenched, as the hunters' taunts and the injured man's whimpers echoed around the street. She watched him grappled with everything she'd said, the vein on his forehead bulging with adrenaline, until finally he grunted in concession. "Young is right. We move one at a time, starting with you, doc. Keep low and get to the safe house yard. On three," he said.

Charlie shook her head in disbelief. "We may not get another clear shot, we *have* to kill him. He's the head of it all, kill him and the rest will stop!" insisted Charlie.

"It's not a clear shot," said Lopez, peering at the Preacher, who remained in the car, obscured by the cult members moving in front of it, beating the captured man.

"You don't get it, he's the one who killed Petrov," said Charlie, with a crack in her voice.

She grabbed Lucy's pistol and lunged out onto the street.

"Shit!" cried Lucy, reaching after her, but it was too late. Charlie fired at the Preacher.

The hooded figures flinched en masse as the bullet tore past them. It missed the Preacher, but shattered the two front windows of the car. The cult members scattered, taking cover. The driver immediately leapt into the seat, speeding the Preacher to safety.

The remaining robed members opened fire on Lucy's group. Lopez propped his arms on the hood of the car and returned fire, killing one instantly. "You two – *go!*" he ordered.

Lucy grabbed Charlie's arm and heaved her away, wrenching back her pistol as they went. They ducked behind cars and hedgerows as they ran, passing the murdered couple in the yard, and fleeing onto the street beyond. The gunfire stuttered away behind them. Shots were sporadic as both sides strove to conserve ammo.

"Over there!" cried Lucy, spotting an alley.

"This way," called Charlie, at the same moment, racing across the intersection towards a different street, her pace hampered by her sling. Before Lucy could change course, the Preacher's car screeched around the corner and onto the boulevard. Charlie darted between two houses. Lucy sprinted into the alley, and leapt over a fence into someone's back garden. The Preacher's car skidded to a halt and the doors opened.

"You two take the other one, we'll get the doc," cried one of the men.

Lucy ran – hauling herself over garden fences, and fleeing deeper into the suburbs, as gun shots continued to ring out from Lopez's street.

***

The light was fading. Lucy's legs were weak. She'd trekked for hours, desperately evading the Faithful as she sought out her last glimmer of hope; her mother. She stowed the stolen city map away in her backpack as she read the street name before her: *Carlton Avenue*. This was it; the address the agency had mailed her all those months ago.

The houses were narrow, terraced affairs, made of red brick. Aside from that the street was like every other; deserted. After months of dreaming about her, of planning this moment, Lucy felt hollow.

She approached the door and took a deep breath, trying to suppress her flickering hope. She knocked several times. No answer. She looked around for a spare key but there was none. Raising her pistol, she took careful aim and fired at the lock, blasting it open. The gunshot reverberated around the silent streets. She pushed the door open.

The hall was filled with unopened mail. *Final notice. Payment due. Do not ignore.* Almost half of the envelopes bore the same bold print. The rest was a mixture of high fashion catalogues and lifestyle magazines. The mail was addressed to different people. *Mrs. Edelstein, Ms. Sanchez, Rosemary Carter, Mrs. Walker.* Then finally, one Lucy recognized: *Tessa Young*.

She picked it up and stared at the writing. There she was. Her mother. The letter was for an unpaid parking fine. That would figure.

Lucy moved further into the house. The level of dishevelment was immediately familiar. Discarded clothes, magazines and used crockery occupied every viable surface including the floor. Beneath the detritus Lucy identified a sofa, a bean bag, and a large reclining armchair. Books were stacked up in piles by each – holiday reads, chick flicks, detective stories. The floor was covered in short pale hairs, as were the sides of a tattered dog basket in the corner. It looked large enough to take a Labrador. Knowing her mum, it had probably housed a husky.

A wrinkled blanket lay at one end of the sofa, along from a bedroom pillow, which was propped against the opposite arm. Lipstick and makeup cluttered the coffee table, which was stained with rings from hot mugs. A collection of three different-sized Yankee candles held the central position.

Lucy headed upstairs to explore the top floor. It was in a similar state of disarray, decorated in clothes, makeup, and books. The master bedroom featured an un-made double bed. A torn condom wrapper lay on the carpet. Near it lay a lighter and an ash tray brimming with cigarette butts. Lucy pocketed the lighter, which worked, and kicked the condom wrapper under the bedframe, wincing as she did so.

She opened the wardrobe. None of the clothes were familiar, but she recognized her mother's style. Subtlety had never been her forte. The woman was a great believer in the adage 'more is more'. Lucy pulled out a selection of clothes – jeans, a t-shirt, a long-sleeved jersey, and some thick socks – and laid them out on the bed. She unzipped the top of her uniform, then reconsidered; it had been days since she'd washed properly.

She took herself to the bathroom and inspected the shower. Lime scale water marks gave the glass screen a mottled appearance. A mass of long black hair clung to the drain. The cubicle floor was grimy, too. Lucy grimaced and checked the sink instead. It had a hairline crack, and large orange stain around the plug hole. She tried the tap but nothing came out, so she turned her attention to the toilet instead. Cautiously, she lifted the cistern lid off, remembering the twitching tadpoles she'd seen in the semi-frozen house by Madison.

The cistern was full, and the water was clear. Lucy fetched a glass from downstairs and scooped some out, quenching her thirst. She stripped off, removing her well-worn uniform and sweat-stained base layer. She took a flannel from the towel rail and squeezed soap into it from the dispenser, then tipped some of the glass's water onto it. She cleaned herself briskly in the chilly house. As she scrubbed, she marveled at her skin – there was no trace of the lesions. All that remained were scratches and bruises from her escape.

She dried herself with a towel, then returned to the bedroom where she quickly changed into her mother's clothes. The thick socks felt luxurious against her aching, blistered feet. She slid on a pair of slippers, threw a dressing gown over her whole outfit, and headed downstairs, with a fresh cup of water.

She drew the curtains, then searched the house for food. She didn't bother opening the fridge – remembering the rancid smell of the farmhouse's abandoned unit. Instead she checked through each empty cupboard in turn, until her eyes fell on the dog bowl. Lucy knelt down before her last hope: the cupboard under the sink. To her joy she discovered a box of dog biscuits. She shoveled several down on the spot, savoring the crunchy, calorie-filled nourishment, groaning with pleasure as she chomped.

She carried the box into the lounge, where she lit the Yankee candles, then sank into the sofa, clutching the box like it was popcorn. The treats tasted better than she'd expected – certainly no worse than the leaves. She gorged until she could eat no more, then let out a dog-food-flavored belch.

She finished the water and placed the empty cup on the floor, beside a pile of books. Next to it, she noticed a pen. She reached under the sofa and groped around until her hand landed on a hidden volume, which she pulled out. The cover had no text, just a polka dot pattern of gold on fluorescent pink. Lucy opened a random page and recognized her mother's handwriting immediately. The entry was over nine months old.

8th June. Went to Cindy's today, as per, and this new bitch at the mall asked me for ID when I tried to pay by check. I was like 'excuse me?', and she was like 'yeah?' I informed her of her error – I am a loyal *customer. They should put that in the friggin training manual. The manager came over, all embarrassed, and was like 'Ms Sanchez, forgive my colleague, she's new here, of course we don't require ID from you,' and I was like 'damned right you don't.' Normally I'd have given them a piece of my mind – otherwise how else are they gonna learn? – but I had a lunch date I simply could not miss, and the jacket was very cute, so I needed it in a hurry, obviously.*

Lucy skipped to the last entry in the book, hoping to find some clue as to her mother's fate.

2nd September. Jacob's a piece of shit. I told him I don't have the money, but he gives me all this bull crap about his rights, and I told him to go get a lawyer if he felt that strongly about it, which he won't, because he doesn't, because the man couldn't feel strongly about something if his life depended on it. He's got zero backbone. Like, zero.

She thumbed through the diary, drinking in snapshots of her mother's second life; the one she'd left Lucy for. It spoke of people, and boyfriends, creditors and lawyers, job interviews and tribunals, parties and breakups. Lucy kept reading, hoping desperately to find something concrete – the reason her mother left, perhaps, or even some mention of herself, but the entries were vacuous and self-absorbed, and all Lucy found was sleep.

***

Lucy squeezed her way between the adult guests' legs until she reached the bar. "Excuse me, mister, can I get a cream soda?" Lucy shouted, straining over the music her parents liked. The bartender tapped the sign above his head. *Over-21s only.* "Please?" added Lucy. The man let out a sigh and poured her a glassful. He slid it across, with a frown, then shoed her away quickly as his supervisor returned.

The music stopped mid-track and the DJ's voice wafted through the microphone. "Uh-oh, looks like someone's gonna have to make a speech!" he declared, in a voice so cheesy it could've curdled the very room.

The cry of "speech!" echoed around the packed bar as tipsy guests demanded a turn from the birthday girl. Tessa feigned reluctance, then skipped onto the stage and plucked the mic from the DJ's podgy hands. Lucy's mom was wearing a cowboy hat and a checkered shirt, with the center tied in a knot to show off her slender midriff.

"Thank y'all soooo much for coming," Tessa gushed, before taking a moment to giggle, and pick out several faces in the crowd. "Any of y'all that said I wouldn't make it to thirty? Y'all owe me five bucks," she said, to the crowd's delight.

Lucy felt two hands scoop her up. Now she was sat on her dad's shoulders, with full view of the room.

"There's my baby! What would I do without you and my boo? Y'all are my superstars and I love ya," gushed Tessa, waving at them. Lucy waved back, grinning goonishly.

"Don't tell me they get all your love," added the DJ, playfully, having found a second mic.

A few wolf whistles from the crowd, to which Tessa feigned outrage, declaring publically her undying affections for her family.

A cake appeared from the far side of the room and the crowd launched into a rowdy rendition of *Happy Birthday*, as a giant, iced three and zero, studded in candles, processed to the front. Tessa blew them out to the crowd's applause, and the music resumed. She jumped down from the stage and launched into some energetic dancing.

Lucy's father steered Lucy away and left her to play with the other children. A neighbor brought them all some cake a while later. The icing was sickly sweet. Lucy wolfed down two fat slices in quick succession. They made her thirsty, but she didn't care for the kids' table orange aid – she wanted cream soda.

She squeezed her way through the forest of adult legs once again. She weaved across the train station platform and marched to the front of the bar. The bartender was busy this time, rushing from end to end, grabbing bottles off the shelves and up-ending them, pouring splashes into glasses then adding ice and sodas. She waved, but he wouldn't make eye contact.

"There you are baby!" cried Tessa.

Her mom drew her into a fierce embrace, shielding Lucy from the rushing wind as a freight train sped by. Tessa propped Lucy against her hip in a koala grip and gave her daughter a beaming smile, as she swayed to the bar's music. Lucy's face lit up and the two of them giggled at each other.

"Sweetie, I've been looking for you alllll night, where's my baby been?" cooed her mom.

"Playing," giggled Lucy, pulling a breathing mask over her mouth.

"Playing, huh? Wish I could be playing. I gotta talk to all these boring adult people. You wanna swap?" whispered her mom, conspiratorially.

"No," giggled Lucy, behind the mask.

"What you doing up here anyways? Is someone rooting for another cream soda?" said her mom, with a wink.

Lucy nodded, grinning.

"Cream soda for my baby, and a JD coke for her momma," declared Tessa, tapping the bar with her knuckles. "You are just my world, you know that honey? You're my *world*." Tessa nuzzled Lucy's neck with her nose. It tickled, making Lucy giggle further, as she bathed in the scent of her mother's perfume.

***

Lucy awoke sharply. There was a voice outside the window. Daylight shone through the crack in the curtains.

"Son of a bitch, I *knew* I should've come sooner. Check it – someone's broke in."

The voice outside belonged to a woman.

Lucy leapt up from the sofa. The blanket and her mother's diary fell off her as she dashed to the far side of the room, grabbing her pistol as she moved. She crept to the lounge door and waited behind it. The stranger shoved the front door open, dislodging Lucy's improvised door-stopper in the process. Footsteps marched across the hallway and towards the lounge.

"Don't move," said Lucy, levelling the pistol at the woman's head as she entered the room.

The stranger was around twenty years old. She raised her arms in immediate surrender, her eyes wide with fear.

"Please don't kill me," the young woman begged. Then her mouth slackened, and her arms faltered. She stared at Lucy in disbelief. "Oh my god – it's you. You're… you're Lucy," said the woman.

Lucy's jaw dropped, but she kept the pistol raised.

"I'm Shona," said the woman, lowering her hands further. "I'm your sister."

SIX

Blood

Lucy lowered the pistol. "I don't have a... How do you...?"

"I'm your half-sister. Mom showed me pictures of you," said Shona.

"When?" said Lucy.

"Before she – before the virus," said Shona.

"So she's dead?" said Lucy.

Shona nodded. Lucy lowered the pistol and slumped into the armchair.

"May I?" said Shona, gesturing to the couch.

"Of course," said Lucy, waving her through, and setting the pistol down on the coffee table. "Sorry about the gun. Life's – you know. What happened to mom?"

"She died in the first week. It was the virus that got her. I buried her properly. We can visit the grave if you want. I'm so sorry – you've come all this way, this must be so awful. How did you even make it here from Louisiana?" said Shona.

"I'm from San Francisco," said Lucy, matter-of-factly.

"Oh, sorry. Mom said Clinton," said Shona.

"Clinton's where she left us," said Lucy, staring at the coffee table.

"Are you on your own?" said Shona.

Lucy laughed once, bitterly. "Yeah Shona, I'm on my own," she replied.

"It's not safe to be alone in this city. Please, come back with us – we have food, and hot water, and so much to talk about I don't even know where to begin," said Shona.

"We?" said Lucy.

"Hey Troy, come say hi," called Shona, leaning into the hallway.

A car door slammed outside and footsteps approached the building, crossing the threshold, and the short hall.

"Troy, you're not gonna believe this – it's some kinda miracle – this is my sister, Lucy," said Shona, beaming.

A tall, well-fed man entered the room, with a shotgun slung over his shoulder. He wore a sweeping robe of brilliant white. A bronze medallion hung from his neck by a crimson cord. Lucy gasped.

"Lucy, this is my partner, Troy – though most people call him Preacher," said Shona.

"That your pistol, ma'am?" said Troy, to Lucy, aiming the shotgun at her.

"Uh, yeah," said Lucy, gulping, her eyes flitting to her discarded pistol on the coffee table.

"Shona sweetie, would you pick it up for me?" said Troy, his voice stern.

"Troy, this is so rude, she's my sister!" said Shona, fetching the pistol.

Troy pocketed the pistol, and slung the shotgun over his shoulder, giving Lucy a smile of genuine warmth.

"Sorry about the hostility, Lucy, but times have changed. I'm hoping they'll change back. It's an honor to meet you. If you've got half your sister's genes, then that makes you half perfect. I wanna be clear – you're family, and that means you'll always have a place at our table. Break bread with us and shelter with us as long as you need," he said, with a gracious bow.

"Uh, thank you," said Lucy, her stomach churning. She looked nervously at Shona, who was smiling, proudly.

"Did you find the photos, honey?" said the Preacher.

"Gosh, I totally forgot, lemme grab them," said Shona, rootling through the cupboards.

"We got a limited number of vehicles, so I keep trips like this on the DL – otherwise folk get jealous, you know? And fairness is a big thing, now," said Troy.

"Oh, sure," said Lucy, watching as Shona scooped up all the photos in the room. She knew exactly which drawers to check.

"That's all of them," said Shona.

"OK sweetie, let's make a move. Lucy, how did you get here – you got a car?" said Troy.

"Uh, it broke down south of the city. I walked here," she said, swallowing nervously.

"She started in San Francisco," added Shona.

"That's a long way. To make a journey like that, in times like these? That's real love. I think it makes you something of a pilgrim, Lucy. Come on now, let's get home – this calls for a celebratory lunch. We shall mark the pilgrim's arrival," said Troy, warmly.

***

As they drove across town it became clear they were entering the Faithful's territory. Many of buildings they passed had long black sheets billowing from the uppermost windows, trailing down several floors. They'd even reached two skyscrapers. At ground level, gone were the black painted crosses on street corners – there were no infected streets here. In their place was a new emblem: a painted white ring with a horizontal line through the middle.

They were in the historic quarter of the city. Centuries-old stone buildings stood nestled among their taller, glass descendants. At every checkpoint they passed, the guards would pay their respects to Troy with great sincerity. He would offer them a blessing – words of encouragement and love – and introduce Lucy, 'their newest pilgrim'.

Finally, they came to a stop. *One McKinley Square* read the inscription above a stately building. The square was bustling with people moving between buildings, ferrying carts of water, bread, laundry, books, wood, tools. Everyone seemed to have a clear purpose. Only a handful of patrolling men and women with guns wore black robes. But the guns were holstered, or slung over shoulders, and the guards engaged in convivial conversation with their non-uniformed peers.

Lucy climbed out of the car, with the others. She could smell the sea. She took in the tall, imposing stone building opposite. *Mariott's Custom House* read the inscription. The front featured broad, neo-classical stone pillars several stories high, adorned by a temple-like triangular pediment. Out of this rose a stone tower easily two dozen stories high. It was clad in billowing black sheets bearing the white emblem.

"This way," said Shona, taking Lucy by the arm and steering her towards the first stately building. It was seven stories high, and had a dozen windows spanning the width of the building. Each was inset among wide stone walls, with decorative touches of masonry. A band of stone cornicing wrapped around the upper floors of the building, culminating in an elliptical archway that drew the eye towards the center of the building.

Shona led the way inside. Much of the ground floor office space had been converted into a canteen, where the three of them took a seat. The Preacher was immediately beset with questions from fellow workers, so Shona took Lucy to the buffet, where they each received a portion of hot, smoked fish and corn bread. Shona took a portion for the Preacher, too.

They retook their seats. Troy invited Shona to say grace.

"My Preacher, my brothers and sisters, for this gift we thank you, and by the grace of the Almighty, we will prevail," she said, scrunching up her eyes in concentration as she delivered each syllable with sincerity.

"Together," said the Preacher, raising his cup of water.

"Together," said Shona, smiling. She raised hers, and intimated to Lucy to copy. The three clinked glasses and ate.

The Preacher was keen to know details of Lucy's journey so far. She gave an honest account of the creatures, and the train, her loss of Dan, and her struggle to survive the winter alone. She told them of the military, and the Queen in NYC, but stopped short of any mention of the white powder disease. The Preacher listened intently, and pressed her for details about the D4 creatures that were plaguing the rest of the country.

"From your accounts, Lucy, I believe spring will bring us these creatures, and they will be our greatest test yet. I must humbly ask you to help us prepare for this. With your knowledge, and the Lord's wisdom, we can protect my people from this threat," he said, solemnly.

Shona nodded eagerly in approval, and looked to Lucy, expectantly. Lucy muttered an awkward pledge to help in any way she could.

"We're being punished for our arrogance," continued Troy.

"Amen," said Shona, nodding further.

"First God sent us the virus. Those who repented, and those whom She chose, survived. Then came Her winter, and with it the justice of nature. Nature exists to teach us humility, Lucy. With the first thaw, God sent Her messengers to me, who told of the state of the city. I knew I could not sit idly by and allow such barbarism to persist. I looked into my heart and I felt the love of the Lord and I answered Her call. We eradicated the unspeakables, Lucy. We saved this city from its descent into savagery, and the gravest of carnal sins. But there is work yet to be done. There is a new scourge in this city, and we must punish the sinners. We will track them down, one by one, and cleanse their souls in the name of the Lord. But our work will not end there, Lucy. Spring is coming, and with it, there will be a day of reckoning for those who have abandoned their fellow human. For the police, holed in up in their prison fortress, and for the dispassionate, hiding behind their walls. Justice will come to them, Lucy, the Lord's justice. And the weak, the vulnerable, those who kept their faith, and those who have found it, they will become the strong. Theirs is the future, Lucy. And so it will be done," said Troy.

***

"Are you ready?" said Shona, knocking on the door.

Lucy's apartment was beautiful. It had been a hell of a climb to reach the fifteenth floor of the Mariott's tower, but the view of the city was incredible. She had luxurious bedding, a candle to read by, and a choice of books from the hotel library.

"Just a minute," said Lucy, as she changed out of her work clothes. The smell of fish lingered in them after an afternoon of gutting, de-boning, and smoking that day's haul. She froze as she caught sight of her back in the mirror. A fresh lesion had appeared between her shoulder blades. It looked raw, and was already the width of her fist.

A church bell sounded three times.

"We don't want to be late," said Shona, tapping at the door again.

"Nearly there," called Lucy, as she tugged on her shirt, firmly, along with a jumper and woolly hat.

"How do I look?" she said, opening the door to Shona.

"They fit you so well!" cheered Shona, who had lent her the clothes so that she'd have a non-work set.

Lucy's face fell. Shona was wearing a black robe.

"Wow, you've got one of those huh?" said Lucy, trying to contain her disgust.

"And now so do you!" chimed Shona, proudly whipping out a spare robe from behind her back.

"This is for me?" said Lucy, holding the garment at arm's length.

"You'll need it, you're not allowed in church without one. We actually don't have enough right now, but there are lots of masses every day, so people share them. I pulled a few strings – got you a good one," said Shona, with a playful nudge.

"Uh, thanks," said Lucy.

The bell sounded again: three chimes at one-second intervals.

"Quick, put it on," said Shona, helping Lucy into it. "It totally suits you! Let's go – we don't wanna be stuck in the back row," she added, setting off excitedly.

As they descended the staircase, they joined a growing trickle of robe-clad residents, all heading to the central conference room in the building across the square. At the door, every resident was patted down by the ushers.

"No weapons allowed inside the church," whispered Shona, explaining.

Lucy winced as the usher patted her lesion. She followed Shona inside the crowded room. The first two rows were full already, but Shona squeezed them into the third.

"I know what you're thinking," whispered Shona.

Lucy raised an eyebrow.

"How comes the Preacher's partner doesn't get a front row seat? We're all equal in the eyes of the Lord, Lucy," said Shona, with a chuckle.

Within five minutes the conference room was packed. There was an excited murmuring across the hundred or so robe-clad residents, but with the sounding of a gong, they all fell silent and rose to their feet. Lucy copied, and watched as Troy strode onto the stage, his white robe glimmering in the candlelight.

"Sisters, brothers, friends, a blessed evening to you all," he boomed.

"And to you, oh Preacher," replied the crowd.

"Be seated, please. Tonight, I have joyous news. The Lord, in Her infinite wisdom, has delivered unto us a lesson," declared Troy.

"Hallelujah!" cried Shona, with dozens of others from the crowd, all on the edges of their seats.

"We know that the Lord is true to us. She guides us, and we will follow. For those who follow prosper!" said Troy.

More cries of confirmation from the crowd.

"We have been chosen by the Lord. Chosen to survive, chosen to take Her message to the others; to Her children who have strayed from the path of righteousness. She chose *us* to survive the virus, She chose *us* to survive the winter, She chose *us* to defeat the unspeakables," shouted Troy.

"Amen, amen, amen!" cheered the crowd.

"But now, my faithful children, the Lord has tasked us once again. She has marked out those who have forsaken her, those who have sinned and continue to sin. She has put upon them a plague, a sickliness, to punish their arrogance and their folly. It is on us, as Her instruments on this Earth, to complete this work She has so wisely begun. Will you let the Lord guide your spirit? Will you open your heart to Her wisdom? Will you be a vessel for Her work?" cried Troy.

"We will!" replied the crowd, in forceful unison.

"My brothers and sisters, some of you have seen this curse first hand. Others of you have heard me speak of it. The scourge. The plague. The sickness. It is the Lord's work. She has marked out those whom we must cleanse, and cleanse them we shall. But there is a second, more heinous group of sinners we must also address. Those who chose to deny the Lord's will!" declared Troy.

"Arrogance! Shame! Blasphemy!" cried the crowd.

"Incredible as it may seem, there are those who deny the Lord's curse. They seek to *reverse* it. They seek to *deny* it. They seek to challenge the Lord's *wisdom*. As if their judgement is superior! This is an affliction worse than the plague itself. It is a form of blindness. It is pure sin. My children, I must tell you solemnly, that tonight, we have such a sinner in our midst!"

The crowd reacted with shock and dismay. Frenetic murmuring broke out. A chill of dread washed over Lucy.

"Indeed! It is a terrible thing! But it is the truth! The Lord has delivered into our hands an agent of Satan!" declared Troy.

The crowd cried out for punishment, for retribution, for justice. Lucy looked nervously to Shona who, beside her, was punching the air, echoing her peers' cries for blood. She turned and gave Lucy a beaming smile, then carried on cheering.

"Tonight, we will *be* the Lord's witnesses. Tonight, we will *see* the Lord's judgement. Tonight, we will *do* the Lord's work!" declared Troy, to the crowd's cheers.

He raised his hand and two robed ushers dragged a prisoner to the center of the stage. The person was dressed in a khaki jumpsuit. Their hands were bound behind their back, and their head covered by a hood. Lucy's heart froze. The ushers thrust the figure onto their knees, facing the crowd. Troy marched to the side of the prisoner and paused, with his hand hovering above the prisoner's head. In an instant, he snatched the hood off.

The crowd rose to their feet and erupted with jeers of hate and condemnation. Lucy stared in horror, as Troy circled the doctor. Charlie stared at the crowd in disbelief and fear, and shook her head imploringly as they taunted her with cries of "Sinner!"

Troy clapped his hands and the crowd fell silent, retaking their seats.

"My brothers and sisters, our Lord is just. Our Lord is wise. But is our Lord not also merciful?" said Troy.

Murmurs of consent among the crowd.

"Is our Lord not also love?"

A few cries of "Amen" answered the call.

"If we are to rebuild our world with humility, and the love of the Lord in our hearts, we must be prepared to forgive. As many of you in this very room have been forgiven, so too must you be willing to forgive others. But ultimately, forgiveness is the Lord's to give. And to be forgiven, you must first *ask* the Lord to forgive you. So here we are, my children. I give you this sinner, before the Lord. I pray that she repents. I pray that she searches her heart for truth. I pray that she begs the Lord, here and now, for forgiveness," declared Troy.

All eyes fell upon the doctor, whose eyes were filled with tears.

"Speak, child, for the Lord is listening," urged Troy.

"I'm begging everyone in this room to remember who they were before this happened. Think of what you knew! Think of what you had! Technology, medicine, electricity! This insanity is not the way back, remember who you *are*!" implored Charlie.

The crowd stared at her silently, while Troy circled with slow, careful paces.

"Is that your final word?" he asked.

"How is this happening? I've committed no crime, I'm a *doctor*. Remember those? The people that kept everyone alive? All I'm doing is helping sick people," pleaded Charlie.

"You are denying the will of the Lord. You are abetting sinners. That makes you a sinner, too," said Troy.

"I'm the sinner? You killed my partner. He was unarmed! You're a god damned *murderer*," she cried.

The crowd booed and jeered in outrage at this insult to their leader, with some in the front row spitting at Charlie.

"There you have it. Her final word. No humility, no repentance, instead she accuses the Lord's servants. This sinner has refused forgiveness. Justice must be delivered!" cried Troy.

The crowd cheered eagerly as the ushers dragged Charlie from the room. The fire exit doors were opened, and the congregation poured outside into McKinley square, where guards stood with large, burning torches.

The night was clear, and the moon was almost full. The ushers wrestled the doctor into the center of the square, then backed away as the congregation encircled her. More robe-wearers circulated through the crowd, wheeling a cart of jagged rocks and bricks.

"Take one," instructed Shona, eagerly, as she took two herself.

Lucy picked up a small, sharp stone, and held it limply by her side. A sickening feeling rose through her stomach.

"Do we have any new believers?" cried Troy, as he entered the center of the circle.

"Here!" cried Shona, taking Lucy by the hand and pulling her to the front. A few others also made their way forwards, including a parent, dragging her young daughter. The girl looked too young to even start school. The newcomers looked nervously at one another. A few stared at the doctor with grim determination.

Charlie spotted Lucy and the pair locked eyes. Lucy swayed, her hand trembling. She glanced around the courtyard, searching for a way to intervene, looking for a gun to grab – something, *anything*. The doctor gave her a micro-shake of the head and stared at the ground, then closed her eyes. Troy stepped back from the condemned woman and addressed the crowd with fervor.

"Tonight, you are all instruments of the Lord. You are agents of Her justice! Do you feel Her *spirit* working through you?" he bellowed.

"We do!" cried the crowd.

"Do you feel her *power* working through you?" demanded Troy.

"We do!" cried the crowd, louder still, including many of the newcomers in the front row.

"Are you prepared to deliver the Lord's our savior's *justice*?" cried Troy.

"We are!" proclaimed the crowd. The child, buoyed by her mother's encouragement, was also shouting, and looking upon the doctor with hatred.

"Then I say to you, in the name of the Lord, let Her will be done!" declared Troy.

The crowd erupted in cries of anger and condemnation, as they unleashed a barrage of rocks and bricks upon the kneeling doctor. The stones pulverized Charlie's body, swiftly sending her to the ground. The crowd pressed in further, crushing around Lucy, as they hurled stones directly down upon her, bludgeoning the doctor's face, splitting open her skull, rupturing her organs.

The worshippers jostled and cheered, all eager to ensure they contributed to the work of the Lord. Lucy dropped her stone and ran from the crowd. She staggered to a bench in the square and vomited heavily, before collapsing, weeping.

After less than a minute, the commotion was over, and the crowd cheered in celebration. Shona appeared by the bench and knelt beside Lucy. Her voice was tender but energized.

"Hey, you did a good thing, I was scared the first time, too, but once you've let the Lord into your heart, you'll see it's OK. That awful woman's free now. Her soul has been saved," said Shona, stroking Lucy's hair.

Another voice drew Lucy's head up, as the newcomer mother crossed the square, holding her daughter's hand. "I am *so* proud of you. The Lord is gonna be *so* impressed by what you did," said the child's mother.

Lucy glanced up at the center of the square, where a sheet had been drawn over the doctor's mutilated body. Ushers were busily spraying the site with holy water and muttering incantations.

Troy strolled over to the bench and took a seat beside Lucy.

"I abhor violence. I always have, and I always will. But sometimes, when we are doing the will of the Lord, we must sacrifice our own feelings, for something much greater than ourselves. You understand why this was necessary. You are a woman of science yourself, Lucy. You know we cannot rebuild mankind if we allow this sickness to invade us. You are one of us now, Lucy. And the Lord has a plan for you," said Troy.

Marcus Martin

SEVEN

Mother

It had been three days since the execution. Lucy's lesions were spreading, radiating across her torso. She was feeling weaker, and knew the dizziness would start soon. It was only a matter of days before the lesions spread to her hands and face. She found herself craving the fermented leaves, and had to force down her fish and corn meals to keep up appearances.

It was impossible to leave the company of others without arousing suspicion. Shona, who doted on her with great affection, was by her side almost every hour of the day, and had been proudly introducing her to the rest of the community one by one. There was simply no way for Lucy to seek out medicine without arousing suspicion, and time was running out.

She'd spent the past three days rotating through various chores that kept the community running. As a newcomer, her scope was limited to basic tasks, from fetching water, to preparing food, repairing garments and stoking fires. She knew there were research teams, but they were chemists and engineers, urgently trying to figure out a viable fuel source now that the city's gasoline had all but run dry. She'd spoken to a couple of them over dinner. They were trying to convert the building's generator to run off biomass, but the prototypes so far had been unsuccessful. Nonetheless, each professed their commitment to restore mankind to its technologized glory, in the name of the Lord. Knowledge was a gift from above, after all, and it was their duty to preserve that gift and ensure it was used. To do otherwise, they argued, would be to disrespect Her will.

The Preacher was absent. His prayers had instructed him to conduct a hunt for sinners in the western outskirts of the city. He'd taken a team of volunteers and veterans, declaring that they would penetrate further than before, and comb through the streets over several days. The hunting party was expected back the following evening.

Shona had chosen to share a secret with Lucy on the first night of the Preacher's absence: she was pregnant with his child. Shona could barely contain her excitement, which made up for Lucy's emotionally stunted response. Shona insisted that she didn't want to tell anyone else, especially not the Preacher, until another month had passed, just so she could be sure, but she felt certain, and was convinced it would be a girl.

The period of the Preacher's absence was marked by tranquility. Masses were held in his absence, led by devout members from Preacher's original farming community. There was no dissent. The community regulated itself with incredible calm and dignity. Disputes were settled by a senior cleric, who would arbitrate in the Preacher's absence. Violence was unnecessary, because the residents were all there by choice, and were equally invested in the success of the community.

March 7th (est.) – The people here are showing me immense kindness. I have quickly seen the love between them, and the peace they are striving for. Through the Preacher's wisdom, I hope the Lord rids us of the plague in the city, and that the souls of those affected are redeemed through Her justice.

Lucy had taken to writing fictitious entries in her diary, lest anyone from the community read her notes. The community was awash with smiles, kindly words, and hawkish eyes. It was imperative they believed Lucy was faithful, if she was going to survive. She couldn't risk anyone calling her into question, and a religious court demanding to inspect her skin. Similarly, she'd amended any diary entries referring to her use of white powder, by rewriting them obliquely so that they would only make sense to her.

The community had almost two thousand members, spread across several buildings around McKinley Square. Each building had its own responsibilities for maintaining cleanliness and order, as well as additional specialist functions within the community. Lucy had helped Shona deliver stationery to the school, which operated out of two small conference rooms. The Faithful's school was comprised of two classes, roughly divided into elementary and middle school ages. High school students were allowed to attend in the mornings only, then were required to work in the afternoons and evenings. An ex-teacher and several assisting adults attempted to educate children across all subjects, using their own knowledge, and scavenged textbooks. Lucy observed one of the classes being taught – recent history – which ensured that all children remembered, or learned of, human civilization as it was in the year of 'the great collapse' as they called it. They covered the medical milestones mankind had reached, the incredible opportunities the internet and smart technology had brought, and encouraged children to share memories they had of devices they'd used. The community's core beliefs were woven throughout the curriculum: that mankind had grown arrogant, and that the great collapse was a punishment from above. It was jarring for Lucy to see them discuss the initial epidemic and the collapse of the satellites with a great deal of scientific accuracy, only for them to infuse a narrative of supernatural punishment throughout it. She couldn't deny the motivational element, though; the mantra that they were all chosen survivors, specially selected by the Lord to rebuild mankind from the ashes, proved highly effective. It permeated the whole community. Depression and despair were scant. The bustling district was marked by a sense of optimism, purpose, and hope.

In the evenings, for leisure, the community would provide entertainment from their pool of human talent. On any one night there were musicians, story tellers, crafters, and dancers. Lucy heard the epic tale of the banishing of the cannibals told by two different story tellers. The number of cannibals killed varied wildly between the renditions, but one detail was consistent: the heroic intervention of the Preacher, and the survivors' gratitude to the Lord for sending him.

***

March 7th (est.) – Retiring to bed early again, exhausted after another hard day's work. Shona made me laugh today. I didn't think any good could come from losing mom, but Shona's the exception.

The community here is incredibly positive and nurturing. I'm still adjusting to it – it's not what I've come to expect from life since the great collapse. Hot food, comfortable bedding, clean clothes, even a candle to read by! The engineering team were telling me they've scavenged some photovoltaic cells and are planning on rigging them up for the church and canteen. Their commitment to getting us back on track is inspiring. Were it not for the exhaustion, I think I could maybe be happy here.

The exhaustion was, of course, code for the increasing severity of her symptoms – or the 'scourge', as the Faithful called it. She reflected on her brief entry. To her astonishment, she meant it all. She wondered if, were she not infected, she would have been willing to overlook the barbarism of the Faithful's attitude to the diseased. Perhaps she would have wholly embraced the psychological and physical comforts the community had to offer? For better or for worse, the question was moot. Her condition was worse than ever – the disease was progressing rapidly, and she'd been forced to seek out seated laboring tasks to mask her bouts of dizziness. Her dry, paling complexion was harder to hide, however, and it was only a matter of time before the lesions breached her neckline.

***

A blinding pain woke Lucy, wrenching her from an uneasy slumber. Moonlight shone through a slit in her bedroom curtains. She staggered to the bathroom in agony, clutching her abdomen. It felt swollen. Standing before the mirror, in the pale reflected glow of the moon, she lifted her nightshirt. Her belly button had vanished. Covering her abdomen was a lump the size of a foot. The covering skin looked red-raw. With great trepidation, she pressed her digits upon the swollen area.

The flesh molded around her fingers. She recoiled in horror, but the motion ripped the waxy skin from her midriff. She screamed in pain, then stifled her mouth. She stared downwards. There was no bleeding; the skin that remained was infused with purple. It darkened the closer you got to the center, where the biggest growth was. It throbbed. Lucy felt her hand being drawn to the area magnetically.

She grabbed a flannel and bit down on it. She took several rapid breaths, then pushed her fingers into her malformed abdomen. With a muffled scream, she pierced her own waxy flesh. Her finger tips reached the dark object inside and she wrenched it from her body.

She dropped the mass to the floor; it was a lifeless human fetus. She screamed in horror and recoiled from the room, pressing herself up against the far wall of the bedroom. Her hands trembled with adrenaline, glistening with flecks of her gelatinous, liquid flesh. Her regular abdomen was unaffected, but the ruptured remains of the reddish-purple growth hung from her body like an externalized amniotic sac.

The bedroom door burst open and Shona rushed in, holding a lantern.

"Lucy, are you OK?" she said, setting the lantern on the side and wrapping her sister in a comforting embrace. "I thought someone had hurt you," she soothed.

Shona followed Lucy's eyes to the lifeless, pink form in the bathroom. She gasped in horror, looking from the fetus to Lucy.

She wrenched Lucy's nightshirt up, revealing the ruptured, unnatural flesh.

"Sinner" cried Shona, her eyes filled with fear. "Sinner!" Shona repeated, shouting, this time.

Lucy clamped a trembling hand over her sister's mouth.

"Shh, shh, please, I can explain this, I'm not a sinner, please just be quiet!" begged Lucy, but Shona was petrified, and continued to wail, her cries muffled only by Lucy's hand.

Shona kneed Lucy in the stomach and scrambled to her feet.

"Help! Sinner! Sin-" cried Shona, as she lunged for the door, but Lucy leapt upon her, pinning her to the floor. A wave of renewed strength surged through her body.

Shona scratched at Lucy's face, and kicked with all her might, while Lucy fought to keep her pinned. "Sinner! You're going to hell! Your soul must be cleansed!" spat Shona, with terror in her eyes.

"Shona, please, listen to me!" grunted Lucy, as they rolled violently to the side, knocking into the table. The lantern fell to the floor and smashed. The oil flame spilled out of the glass cage and onto the bed sheets.

"Stone the sinner! Stone her!" groaned Shona, as she clawed her way towards the door, trying to kick Lucy away.

Lucy put a knee into Shona's back. They rolled again, tussling across the smoldering floor. Lucy clambered on top of Shona. She pinned her sister against the floor and covered her mouth, but Shona forced her hand away, and continued her cries. Lucy grabbed Shona's throat in both hands and squeezed with her newfound strength.

"Listen to me, I'm sick, just let me go, I won't come back, but please, *please,* you mustn't tell the others – you know what they'll do to me!" implored Lucy.

Shona's eyes were glazed. She looked at Lucy like she'd never met her before in her life, and kept repeating one single, rasping word. "Sinner!"

Lucy tightened her hands around Shona's neck and squeezed as hard as she could. Her sister's eyes bulged. Her legs flailed and kicked wildly as the last air drained from her lungs. With a final utterance of "sinner!" she fell limp, and her head lolled to the side.

Lucy fell to the ground in exhaustion, but had no time to recover – the bed was ablaze, and the flames had spread to the curtains.

She stumbled over Shona's body. She thrust her notebooks into her backpack, grabbed an armful of essential clothes, and fled the room. She dashed to the emergency stair well. She pulled on the clothes, then raced down the stairs, as cries of alarm echoed out from her floor as the incident was discovered. She hurtled down the fifteen floors, jumping five steps at a time until she reached the bottom. Panting, she drew her coat around her, creasing up in pain as her damaged, secondary abdomen pulsated. The brief surge of strength was fading. She could feel her limbs weakening. Dizziness was crashing down upon her. Shouts echoed from atop the stairwell. Groaning in pain, she kicked open the exit, and stumbled out into the night.

Marcus Martin

The epic story concludes in

ASH

Convulsive Part Four

Available now at

www.marcusmartin.co.uk

and

www.amazon.com/author/marcusmartin

Enjoy this book?

You can make a big difference

Reviews are like oxygen for new authors. As a self-published, indie author, I don't have the wealth of a huge publishing or PR firm behind me. I depend on amazing readers like you to help spread the word about my work.

If you've enjoyed this book, I would be tremendously grateful if you could take a couple of minutes to leave me an honest review (it can be as short as you like).

With sincere thanks for your support and commitment – Marcus.

ABOUT THE AUTHOR

Marcus Martin began his writing career creating dramas and comedies for theatre and radio, before expanding into the world of books. He is also an avid composer and songwriter. He's currently based in Cambridge, UK, where the buildings are old, the science is pioneering, and the trees are plentiful.

Join my mail list
Stay up to date on the next releases, get insights into my writing process, and get exclusive advanced reader copies of future books.

www.marcusmartin.co.uk

ALSO BY MARCUS MARTIN

Have you read them all?

In the Convulsive **Series**

Lucy's epic journey takes her into the heart of the apocalypse. The creatures are closing in, and every decision is life or death. But survival comes at a cost…

CRISIS

GRIT

TRIBES

ASH

In Trios: Three short stories

Looking for something completely different? Try these short stories by Marcus Martin. Surreal, slapstick, and satirical. Palate cleansers for the eclectic reader.

THE FLOOD

SLIGHT HITCH

GOOD IDEA, CAESAR!

Become a

superfan.

Become a superfan from just $1 per month.

Join the awesome community and support my next creative project.

www.patreon.com/marcusmartin

Printed in Great Britain
by Amazon